PROMISE KEPT

JODI ALLEN BRICE

CHAPTER 1

Heather Smith pulled in front of the aging white farmhouse and put the old Chevy Impala in park.

She rubbed her sweaty palms on the nicest pair of jeans she had and tried to calm the nerves fluttering around in her stomach like a multitude of hummingbirds.

She'd spent the last of her cash on gas to drive all the way from Georgia to Mississippi.

She'd forgone getting a hotel and had driven through the night, except to pull over at rest areas and rest her weary eyes.

Everything she owned was in her car.

She killed the engine and stepped out of the car. She slung her backpack over her shoulder.

The white house was cute and homey with a big front porch that looked over the land. She held up her hands and shielded the sun from her eyes and looked over the rolling fields of colors.

She'd never seen so many flowers.

"Are you gonna stand there all day or come on in?"

Startled, she jerked her head back at the house at an old

woman yelling from the front porch. She nodded frantically and hurried toward the house.

"My name is Heather Smith. I'm here for the job." She stopped at the bottom of the steps and looked up at the older woman.

She was wearing a white shirt with oversized overalls and a tan safari hat. Her face was old and weathered, but she looked to be in pretty good health.

"Maybe I have the wrong address?" Heather pulled her phone out of her backpack and punched in some numbers.

"No, honey. You're not at the wrong address." The woman's eyes sparkled with mischief. "My name is Agnes Jackson. I don't live here. Just spending the day with Elizabeth. Can't exactly leave her alone just yet."

"I am not an invalid," a voice called out from in the farmhouse.

Agnes laughed and rolled her eyes. "Come on in, Heather, and let's get you some lemonade. You look plumb tired."

Heather hurried up the steps and tried to catch a glimpse of her reflection in the glass of the door. But Agnes had a hand behind her back, hurrying her inside before she could check herself.

She pressed her hand to her blond hair, smoothed it back, and swallowed the nervousness rising in her throat.

"Come on in the kitchen." Agnes didn't wait for her but continued walking. A honeybee hovered over the woman's hat.

Heather glanced back to make sure the door was shut and no more insects could come inside.

She stepped into an older kitchen that looked like it belonged to a woman who experienced a lot of life. The original hardwood floors had seen their share of scraped knees and spilled spaghetti. The cabinets were oak and the countertops were laminate. There were tiny curtains that hung over the farmhouse sink that looked over the backyard. The counters were clean but cluttered with small appliances and stacks of paper. A white toaster, coffee maker, and Crock-Pot sat along the counter, and judging from their appearance, were well used.

The small oak table was littered with newspapers and some colorful fabric.

"Here, sit on down." Agnes shoved the fabric to the other side of the table and pulled out the chair for Heather. She obligingly sat.

"Where are you from, Heather?" The bee landed on her hat and seemed to be waiting on her answer, as if the insect were interviewing her too.

She stilled at the question. Nowhere.

It was the truth.

She swallowed and plastered on a smile, like she'd been taught. "Georgia."

Agnes turned from the refrigerator and smiled broadly. "Really? What part?"

"Atlanta." She really hoped the woman wouldn't ask any more questions.

"Oh, I just love Atlanta." Agnes poured a cold glass of lemonade and set it down in front of her.

Heather picked up the glass.

"Don't drink that!" A white haired woman hobbled into the kitchen using a walker.

Heather froze, the glass poised halfway to her mouth.

"Well, that's pretty rude, Elizabeth. I expected more out of a Christian woman like you." Agnes scolded. The bee was on the move again and landed on Agnes' shoulder.

Elizabeth moved to the empty kitchen chair and sat down slowly. She sighed and shook her head.

"I didn't make that lemonade. Bertha did." Elizabeth shook her head

"Oh. I see." Agnes grabbed the glass out of Heather's hand and dumped the contents in the sink.

"Who's Bertha?"

"Bertha Billings. One of the women at our church." Elizabeth gave her a slight smile. "She means well but can't boil an egg. She dropped the lemonade off with a pound cake."

"Where's the pound cake?" Agnes frowned. "I didn't see it sitting out with the lemonade when I got here this morning."

"That's because I tossed it out in the backyard." Elizabeth winced and rubbed her hip.

Agnes opened the screen door and peered out. "It's still there. And it's kept its shape. Didn't even break apart when it hit the ground." She looked over her shoulder at Elizabeth. "Wanna bet how long it stays?"

Elizabeth let out a chuckle. "The last time I threw something out she cooked, it took a couple of weeks until a possum came. Didn't eat it, just rolled it away like a tire."

"I bet it was going to make a house out of it." Agnes looked thoughtful.

"Probably. It was hard enough."

Heather snorted. Both women looked at her. She quickly covered her amusement.

"I didn't mean to laugh."

"Why not? It's funny." Agnes sat down and fiddled with the fabrics. "Do you want me to take this to Mattie?" The bee flew around Heather's head. She ducked. It went back and landed on Agnes' strange hat.

Elizabeth sighed. "Please. I meant to do it before I went to have surgery. Since I've gotten home I feel like everything had gone to seed."

"That's why Heather is here. To help you get better so you'll be back on your feet in no time."

Elizabeth turned her astute eyes on her. "You said your

name is Heather Smith? I have to admit I was expecting someone older to apply for the position."

"I'm stronger than I look. I'm a hard worker, and I'll do anything extra that you need. Household chores, cooking. I have experience in helping the elderly recover from surgery."

Agnes barked out a laugh. Elizabeth shot her daggers.

"The last person who called Elizabeth elderly is picking his teeth up off the ground."

Heather's heart squeezed. "I'm sorry I didn't mean any offense."

"It's okay, child. Ignore Agnes." Elizabeth kept her gaze on her. "I heard you tell Agnes you are from Georgia. That's a long way from home. Won't your family miss you? What if you get bored out here in the country with an old lady and her flowers?"

"I won't. I don't have family left." She clasped her hands in her lap. This was her last chance. The last chance she had to have a roof over her head and maybe finally find a home. A real home.

"I put the ad in the newspaper. I didn't think people your age read the newspaper anymore." Elizabeth cocked her head.

"I happened upon it at the library. They put newspapers online."

Elizabeth looked at Agnes. "I didn't know that. Did you, Agnes?"

"Nope. But then again the only thing I use newspapers for is for my garden." The bee made its way to the woman's shoulder.

Heather opened her mouth to warn the woman, but Elizabeth spoke first.

"Heather, do you mind letting me and Agnes speak privately?"

"Not at all." Her stomach was a knot. She stood and

looped the backpack across her shoulder. She headed to the front door and out onto the front porch.

* * *

"Well, Elizabeth, what do you think?" Agnes cocked her head at her friend.

"I don't know. I mean it's not like I'm in a wheelchair or anything." Elizabeth didn't know what to think of the young girl. She hated having to rely on anyone, let alone a stranger.

"Look, you're out of options. You have a farm to run and are just coming off surgery. You need the help. If you don't take her, then Bertha will be over here every day bringing you poison cake." Agnes glared.

Elizabeth snorted. "I don't think it's poison. Just not for human consumption."

"Or animal consumption by the looks of things." Agnes crossed her arms over her ample chest. "Here's what I think."

"Oh my. Here we go." Elizabeth rolled her eyes.

"I think you should hire her. Besides, doesn't the Bible say something about entertaining angels unaware?" Agnes lifted her chin.

"I don't think angels charge a fee," Elizabeth countered.

"Whatever, woman. You know what I mean." She scowled.

"Fine. Tell her to come back inside." Elizabeth sighed.

* * *

Heather felt hot tears rising in her eyes. She blinked them away.

She had hoped to make a better impression on Elizabeth but had failed.

She sat down in one of the wicker rockers by the door.

She heard the women talking but she couldn't make out what they were saying.

She couldn't bear to hear what kind of excuse they would come up with to tell her she wasn't what they were looking for.

The door opened and Agnes poked her head out. "You can come back inside, Heather."

Their conversation was over. It had been too quick. That was a bad sign. She could feel it in her gut.

She stood and followed the old woman inside slowly.

Elizabeth looked up at her with tired eyes. "How about we give it a trial period. Let's say a week."

"Really? I mean yes, thank you." Relief poured through Heather. "I'll work really hard, I promise."

She had her chance at a new life. She had to make sure she didn't blow it.

She just had to make sure her secrets were secure and locked away.

CHAPTER 2

*E*lizabeth motioned for Heather to sit. Agnes poured the tea from the kettle on the stove. "There's a lot to be done here on the farm. And well, I'm old and set in my ways."

"That means she's ornery like a bull," Agnes said happily and took a sip of tea.

Elizabeth narrowed her eyes at her friend. "I've lived here on Harland Creek Farm all my life. After my husband died, I turned it from a cattle farm into a flower farm."

"The farm is named after the town?" Heather took a drink. She wasn't really a tea drinker, but this was really good.

"Yes. My last name is Harland. My great grandfather settled here first. They named the town after him."

"Is there really a creek?" she asked. She'd much rather talk about Elizabeth than herself.

"Yes. Although it's not as big as it once was." Elizabeth smiled. "It runs at the back of my property and separates my farm from the neighbor's farm."

1

"You have a lot of land. I noticed the flowers when I drove up but couldn't tell what kind they were."

"You know anything about flowers?" Agnes leaned forward.

"Not really. But I'm a quick learner." She added the last sentence in a hurry.

"I have different flowers at different seasons. Right now, I have hyacinths, baby's breath, daffodils, and tulips."

"Wow, that's a lot. I noticed how colorful everything is when I drove up. How do you harvest them?" She frowned. Was that even the right word?

"I usually do it. I have some help in the community. Usually hire the high schoolers to help but every year help gets harder and harder to find. The younger people are moving to the big city. Seems like they are wanting out of Harland Creek." Elizabeth's smile didn't reach her eyes. Heather knew the old woman was worried about her future.

"Just like my niece." Agnes sighed heavily.

Elizabeth shook her head. "If I hadn't had surgery, I wouldn't be in this bind."

"Woman, you had to have surgery. You've been putting off getting a new hip for years," Agnes scolded.

"Yes, well, it seems there is never a good time to get old." Elizabeth took a sip of tea and shifted in her seat. Heather caught the wince on her face.

"Are you hurting?" Heather asked.

"I didn't take my pain pill this morning. I was going to do it after the physical therapist came and forgot." Elizabeth rubbed her brow.

Heather stood up quickly and looked around. "Where do you keep it?"

"Over there by the sink."

"By her bag of prunes," Agnes chirped.

"I told you I didn't need you to buy me any prunes." Elizabeth lifted her head.

"When I had my gallbladder taken out, I didn't go for a week. Thought I would blow up like a balloon." Agnes gave her a wide-eyed stare. "I was just looking out for you. You'll thank me later."

Heather bit her lip to keep from laughing. She quickly found a glass in the upper cabinet and filled it with water from the tap. She'd noticed the refrigerator was old and didn't have a water feature. People out here were probably not worried about their water being purified like they worried in the city.

"Thank you, Heather." Elizabeth struggled to open the childproof bottle.

"Here, let me." Heather took the bottle and opened it with ease. She eyed the instructions and poured out one tablet into the older woman's wrinkled palm.

She placed the bottle back where she found it and took her seat.

"How often does physical therapy come see you?" She pulled out a notebook and pen from her backpack.

"Three days a week. Monday, Wednesday, and Friday."

"Do they give you exercises to do on their days off?" Heather scribbled a quick note.

"They want me to walk every day. Not too much, but enough to where I'm not so sore. The physical therapist left a piece of paperwork on the counter."

Heather stood and looked through the paperwork until she found the sheet. She brought it back to the table and nodded.

"She needs help with the housework." Agnes pointed out. "She can't be sweeping and bending down to use a dustpan. And she can't walk upstairs just yet. Thankfully, her bedroom is downstairs."

3

"I can do the housework. And any other errands, like grocery shopping." Heather nodded.

"Heavens, yes. You don't want Bertha bringing more food over here." Agnes grew wide-eyed. The bee made its way up to rest on the top of her hat.

Heather cleared her throat. "Ms. Agnes…"

"Just call me Agnes, dear."

"Agnes, don't be alarmed, but there's a bee on your hat."

She narrowed her eyes at her. "You're not allergic to bees, are you?"

"Not that I know of."

"You're not a bee hater, are you?"

"I don't think so," Heather answered slowly.

"Good." Agnes set her cup down and stood abruptly. "Now that you have some help, I guess I'll be on my way, Elizabeth. I'll run this over to Mildred. I'll find out when the quilting bee is and let you know in case you feel up to it." She gathered up the fabric in her arms. "Now, you call me if you need anything."

"Thanks Agnes." Elizabeth gave her a tired smile but didn't get up.

"Nice to meet you, Heather." Agnes gave her a nod. The bee took flight and followed her out the door.

"I think I'm going to take a nap." Elizabeth slowly got to her feet. Heather stood up beside her in case she needed assistance. "There are three bedrooms upstairs. I'd prefer if you didn't stay in the one with my sewing machine. Too much material spread out everywhere. Once I'm fully healed, I want to get started back on my quilting. You can choose from the other two bedrooms. There's a bathroom across the hall. Go ahead and get your things if you brought them." Elizabeth looked out the window at her car.

"I packed my things in case you hired me. That way I

4

wouldn't have to go back and get them." Truth was, there was nowhere to go back to.

"Good." Elizabeth gave her a look of approval. "I'll let you get settled, and then when I get up, we can start supper and talk about your duties while you are here. I'll show you around the farm as well."

"Ms. Harland?"

"Call me Elizabeth."

"Ms. Elizabeth…"

"Just Elizabeth. No need to add Ms. to it."

"Elizabeth." She nodded. "I need to know if you are allergic to anything. Foods, medicine…"

Elizabeth's eyebrows shot up.

She saw a girl go into anaphylactic shock when she was given a peanut butter sandwich at one time in one of the foster homes she frequented as a child.

"Just one thing. Tomatoes." She slowly made her way back in the direction of her bedroom.

Heather quickly made a note.

She waited until she heard the bedroom door close before heading out to her car and grabbing her meager possessions.

CHAPTER 3

*G*rayson McCade pulled into the parking spot of the Roses and Lace Flower Shop. He'd just finished delivering a few flower arrangements to the hospital. It was his sister's busiest time of year, and he didn't mind helping out when he could manage time away from his farm.

He slid out of his truck and opened the door to the shop.

"Hi, Grayson. I'm just about to order some lunch for me and Olivia. Can I get you something?" Amy Williams smiled behind the counter. She was just the opposite of his sister. Where Amy was outgoing and bubbly, Olivia was shy and reserved. Olivia thrived at arranging flowers into beautiful bouquets and baskets. She hated the marketing part of the florist shop, so she had hired Amy to talk to customers and take orders as well as do the bookkeeping. Olivia preferred to stay in the back, tucked between her coolers full of flowers and making her floral creations.

"Nah, I'm good. I had a big breakfast." He gave the young girl a smile. "Olivia have more deliveries to make today?"

"I think so. I think Sam was on his way over to lend a hand. I tried to tell her I could help with deliveries and making arrangements, but she said she'd rather I stayed out front answering the phones and taking orders." Amy looked a little dejected.

Grayson knew the truth. Amy would drive Olivia mad with her incessant chatter if she were in the back with her. Olivia preferred deep conversations that matter rather than chats about fashion or movie stars or something else that didn't seem to matter.

Amy was a good person. She was just young and had some growing up to do.

"We couldn't run this place without you." He smiled and headed to the back.

Soft sounds of classical music mingled with the scent of roses in the cool space. Olivia spared him a glance when he entered.

"The nurses at the hospital didn't seem to keep you long, I see." She grinned as she worked a long-stemmed red rose into an arrangement.

He groaned. "I told them I was busy."

"You're always busy." She looked at him and continued working.

"A couple of them did ask about you. They wanted me to let you know that there are openings on the med-surg floor. Said they are desperate for more nurses." He opened the cooler and peered inside at their inventory of flowers. She was getting low. Thankfully, the tulip harvest at Elizabeth's was only days away.

Olivia grimaced. "I hope you told them I'm perfectly happy here among my flowers. Besides, not everyone is cut out…"

"I know, I know. Not everyone is cut out to be a nurse." He gave her a sad smile.

She looked up at him. "So, no date tonight? It is Friday, you know."

7

"Too much to do."

"You shouldn't work too much. I know the farm takes up all your time and trying to help me with deliveries is too much to ask of you. I had Amy put an ad in the newspaper for a delivery boy. I'm thinking it would be a good fit for a high schooler. They could make all my deliveries after school."

"Sounds good. Even if you got help, the farm still needs my full attention. Twenty-four seven."

"You should still make an effort to have a social life. You're gonna need a wife to help with that farm." She pointed a rose at him.

"I'm perfectly happy where I am in life, Olivia."

"Grayson, you know Sarah wasn't the right girl for you."

He flinched at the sound of his ex-fiancée's name.

"You need a woman who likes the simple things in life. Someone who isn't always reaching for more."

"I don't know, Olivia. I think it's too soon." He rubbed the back of his neck.

He'd been engaged to Sarah Wilson, his high school sweetheart, for over a year. Until she broke it off a week before their wedding.

He'd been hurt and humiliated. She'd left town to go find herself. She said she'd never lived anywhere but Harland Creek. She wanted to see what else was out there. The truth was, she'd found someone else.

Grayson, on the other hand, could never imagine leaving the town. He liked the comfort of knowing everyone and the countryside that Harland Creek boasted of. Green rolling hills and rain in the spring, and bonfires and deer in the backyard in the winter.

"Stop," Olivia said softly.

"Stop what?" He frowned.

"Thinking about the what-ifs." She waved a stem of baby's breath at him. "You have to move forward, not go backward."

"You're one to talk. You spend every hour here in the flower shop. You haven't had a date in…" He scratched his head and blinked. "Please tell me it wasn't senior prom."

She winced at his words.

"I didn't mean anything by it, Olivia. You know I just want to see you happy."

"I am happy. I have my business and my flowers. And my Brutus when I get off work."

"A German shepherd the size of a horse isn't the kind of companionship I am talking about."

"Sounds like you are deflecting."

"Who's deflecting?" Sam Tucker walked in the back door and let it slam behind him.

Olivia winced at the loud noise. "Sam, tell Grayson that he needs a new girlfriend in his life."

Sam smiled broadly and slapped his hand on Grayson's back. "She's right. You need to get back in the saddle and start dating again."

"I hate when you two gang up on me. I'm fine as I am." He picked up a piece of baby's breath and twirled it in his fingers. One of the nurses just that day had told him he smelled like a meadow.

He was a man; he didn't want to smell like a meadow. And he didn't want women throwing themselves at him, thinking he was desperate.

"I'm sure Sam could hook you up with one of his lady friends."

"You act like I have some black book filled with names." Sam gave her a look of shock.

Olivia stopped working and looked at Sam with mischief in her eyes. "Don't you?"

"Sorry to disappoint but I've been as busy as you, little

mouse." He touched the tip of her nose. She went red at his teasing.

"The only women I've been around are the women at church."

They both stared at him.

He shrugged. "I'm building a new fellowship hall in the back of the church." He patted his stomach. "And they all are trying to fatten me up so no woman will ever want me."

Olivia laughed and shook her head. "Agnes stopped in while you were out. She said she was going over to Ms. Elizabeth's house to sit with her. She said she was going to help her interview a caretaker that had responded to the ad."

"People still take out ads?" Sam frowned and picked up a fuzzy leaf and sniffed. He pulled a face. "This smells like my grandfather."

"It's eucalyptus. And yes. There are people that still read actual newspapers instead of news on their phones." Olivia snatched the branch away.

"I heard she was getting someone to stay with her while she was healing from hip surgery." Grayson frowned. "I need to go over there anyway. I was going to help her harvest some flowers after I see to my cows. Do you have a list of what we need for the shop?"

Olivia nodded and handed him a slip of paper. "I talked to some florists in surrounding cities. They are making a list of what kinds and how many flowers they will need as well. They should get back with me by the end of the week."

Grayson shook his head. "I would hate for her to lose money at her busiest season."

"I know. She's been very fair with her prices. As long as she can get the flowers harvested and delivered on time, she should be okay," Olivia said positively.

"I'll head over in the morning." He stuck the paper in his

jeans pocket. "Oh, and Sam, if you don't want Amy flirting with you, I suggest you head out the way you came in."

Sam flicked a gaze at Olivia and paled. "Thanks for the heads-up. Find out if Ms. Elizabeth needs helps around her farm. I'll try to arrange my work schedule so I can do what I can."

"That's very generous of you," Olivia said. "I know it's hard with her kids living so far away."

"Who would ever want to leave Harland Creek?" Grayson shook his head. "Not me. That's for sure." He nodded to his sister and her best friend and headed back to his truck.

CHAPTER 4

*H*eather woke to sun spilling through her long window. She blinked and looked around the unfamiliar room. Yesterday's memories came flooding back. She was no longer in Georgia anymore. She was in Harland Creek, Mississippi.

She stretched and looked at the clock on the side table. She had slept later than she intended.

She had settled into the smaller room at the end of the hall last night. She'd chosen it because it had more windows for the light to shine through. The walls were wallpapered in a light-blue background with tiny cherry blossoms. There were sheer white curtains that hung on the tall windows.

She liked the light. She'd spent too much of her life in the dark.

Yesterday after Elizabeth had finished her nap, she had helped with supper. She wasn't much of a cook but had helped peel potatoes, and under Elizabeth's instructions, she seasoned the pork chops that had been taken out of the freezer. She took notes when Elizabeth added butter and milk while beating the potatoes until they were rich and creamy. When it came time to make the cornbread, Elizabeth had added the ingredients and let Heather mix them together. Less than thirty minutes later, she was taking golden cornbread out of the oven.

While the meal had cooked, Heather made more notes of ingredients and measurements so she would know how to do it next time. She had caught Elizabeth giving her a strange look. She needed this job more than anything and she wasn't going to mess it up.

By the time supper was done, Elizabeth was too tired to take her out and see the farm. She sat in the living room, watching the nightly news while Heather cleaned up the kitchen. Afterward, she helped Elizabeth get to bed and then went to her bedroom, taking a ziplock bag of crackers and cheese.

Her fingers itched to unpack her small suitcase and backpack she'd brought with her. Every time she tried to pull some clothes out and tuck them in the empty chest of drawers along the wall, she hesitated. She shouldn't get so comfortable. Not yet. She was still on a one-week trial.

After that she could unpack.

And then what?

What would she do once Elizabeth was back on her feet and didn't need her anymore?

She had quickly shoved those thoughts out of her head. She couldn't focus on the future. She just had to get through today.

She sat up, tossed the coverlet off, and stood. The cool hardwood floor felt good against her bare feet. She grabbed her toiletries and headed to the bathroom for a shower.

When she stepped back into the bedroom, she quickly dressed and dried her hair.

As she went down the stairs, she took the time to study the family pictures along the wall. There were pictures of

Elizabeth and her husband and four children. She wondered if the children lived nearby. If so, why were they not here helping their mother recover?

She headed into the kitchen and saw Elizabeth holding on to the sink, trying to make a pot of coffee.

"Please, sit. I'll do that." Heather bit her lip. "I meant to set my alarm but I didn't. I'm sorry. I usually get up around six."

Elizabeth shook her head. "Don't worry about it. I'm sure you were worn out after your drive. I know when Mark takes me to his house, it takes all the energy out of me. I need a vacation after visiting him and his family." She eased into the chair and sighed. She tucked the edges of her robe around her knees.

"Is Mark your son?" She poured water into the coffeepot and measured out the ground coffee.

"He is one of three sons. Jeff and John are my other two. And there's Maggie, my daughter."

"Do they live nearby?"

"Oh no. They all grew up and moved away from Harland Creek. Mark lives in Jackson. And the other three live in Alabama."

"Jackson's not that far from here, is it?" She thought she remembered seeing it on the map.

"Depends on who you ask." There was sadness in the old woman's voice. Heather thought it best to change the subject.

"What do you usually like to eat for breakfast?"

"I usually have just coffee and maybe some toast. I'm not the kind that can jump out of bed and eat. My husband was though. And he wanted homemade biscuits every morning." She chuckled.

Her stomach growled. Embarrassed, she clamped a hand across it.

"There's some cereal in the cabinet and fresh milk in the

refrigerator. I haven't had time to go to the grocery store so we'll make a list today. Add anything you normally eat."

"Anything?"

"Within reason. I don't expect you to pick up filet mignon." Elizabeth shook her head.

"I've never had filet mignon in my life, so I think you're pretty safe." Heather pulled some cups out of the cabinet and found the cream and sugar. She set them on the kitchen table. Her gaze cut to the stack of papers.

"I can go through those and organize them if you want."

"First coffee, then I need to get out to the flowers and see how they are doing."

Heather poured two cups of steaming coffee into the mugs and set them on the table. She slid into the chair across from Elizabeth.

Elizabeth took a sip and smiled. "Good coffee."

"Thanks. It's the one thing I can make." She slammed her mouth shut and looked at Elizabeth.

"It's okay. I figured cooking wasn't your specialty after last night." Elizabeth glanced to the stove. "Just keep taking notes and you'll get better with it in no time."

"What do you normally wear? I can go ahead and lay your clothes out and help you with your shower?" Elizabeth doctored her coffee with creamer and one sugar before taking a drink.

"I can manage my shower by myself. My son had the forethought to update my bathroom a few years ago. He took out the tub and installed a large walk-in shower with a bench."

Heather felt relieved.

"As for my clothes. I usually wear a muumuu."

Heather blinked.

Elizabeth eyed her over her coffee. "You don't know what a muumuu is, do you?"

Heather swallowed.

"It's like a loose dress. A cross between a long shirt and a robe." Elizabeth looked at the laundry room off the kitchen. "I've got some hanging up in there. Just get me whichever one you can get your hands on first."

Heather took a sip and stood. She stepped into the cramped laundry room and saw three large dresses hanging up near the small window.

She picked the pink one with yellow flowers. She walked into the kitchen and spotted some black rubber boots sitting by the back door.

"You usually wear rubber boots when you go out to the flowers?"

"Yes, but my doctor told me to wear tennis shoes until I'm steady on my feet." She narrowed her eyes. "The only shoes I've ever worn are my rubber boots when gardening and my dress shoes for church or going to town." She shook her head.

"Hopefully you'll be healed quickly and you can go back to wearing your rubber boots." Something inside Heather caught. She didn't want to think where she would have to go when Elizabeth didn't need her anymore.

She breathed out a breath and took a sip of her coffee. "I'll lay this on your bed for when you are ready."

"Thank you." Elizabeth cupped her coffee mug in two hands and took a drink.

When Heather got back, she went to the kitchen counter to tidy up the papers.

"Did you sleep well?" Elizabeth looked over at her.

"Yes, I did. Thank you."

"You picked the smaller room at the end of the hall."

Heather looked at her in surprise.

Elizabeth grinned. "It's an old house. I can hear footsteps and I knew you were in Maggie's room." A sad smile crossed her face.

Heather didn't want to press. "I liked how bright the room was. It looks right out onto the field of flowers." She refilled Elizabeth's coffee and topped off her own. She sat down at the table. "It's a lot different environment than what I grew up with."

"Where did you grow up?" Elizabeth pried.

Heather hated lying to the woman. But she wanted and needed this job. Would Elizabeth let her go when she found out she'd been in foster care?

"I…"

The phone let out a shrill ring, and Heather jumped up to answer it. She glanced around the kitchen for the landline.

"In the living room. By my recliner." Elizabeth waved.

Heather hurried and picked up the phone. "Elizabeth Harland residence."

"Well, well, well. Aren't we high and mighty." Agnes snickered on the other end.

"Good morning, Agnes." Heather sighed.

"You're a smart one. Already imprinted my voice on your brain. Good for you, girl. Hey, if Elizabeth kicks you out, can you come over here and answer my phone like that when my ungrateful niece finally calls?"

Elizabeth had made it to the living room and was shaking her head. She held out her hand and Heather gave her the phone. "It's Agnes."

"I know. I could hear her all the way into the kitchen."

"Good morning, Agnes." Elizabeth talked while Heather went and gathered the rest of her clothes. She found the tennis shoes by the bedside table. She gathered a pair of socks and some underwear for Elizabeth. She laid them on the bed and then went back into the kitchen.

Elizabeth was rubbing her head as Agnes prattled on. Heather went into the kitchen and straightened things up before working on the pile of papers on the table and counter. She quickly made two piles. One of bills and important letters and one of junk mail. She found the broom in the pantry and swept up the kitchen floor. She dug out her notebook and pen from her backpack and quickly made a to-do list.

She would assist Elizabeth to get dressed and then help her out to the flower field to check on her flowers. She found a sheet of exercises that Elizabeth was to do on her days when physical therapy didn't come. She looked it over and decided they would do the exercises after they got in from the field. She'd fix lunch and if she had time, run to town for groceries.

She got up and checked under the sink and the pantry, jotting down items she would need. She spotted a worn cookbook on the counter and took it back to the kitchen table.

She opened the worn and colored pages. Her fingers found a pot roast recipe.

"That is my favorite cookbook." Elizabeth eased into the kitchen.

Heather stood up quickly. "I didn't mean to pry."

"Sit." Elizabeth waved her back down. "Since my kids have left, I've not been cooking much. Perhaps look through it and find some recipes you like and we will make them."

She opened the cookbook. "What's your favorite recipe?"

"Fried chicken." She tapped her fingers to the cookbook. "Page 87. That's the best chicken recipe I've ever tried. Do you like fried chicken?"

"Yes. But I usually get it from KFC."

"This is better." Elizabeth smiled. She turned the cookbook where she could see. She thumbed through the casserole section and pointed out some recipes for Heather to try.

Heather quickly jotted down a grocery list of ingredients.

"I've noticed you need some cleaning items. I made a list

while you were talking to Ms. Agnes." She slid the list over to Elizabeth. "Are these what you normally use? If not, I can substitute them."

Elizabeth laughed. "I'm sure what you have down is good enough. After we see to the flowers, then I'll let you run into town for groceries and supplies. I'll go shower and get dressed."

"Do you need help?"

"No, I can manage." She eased toward the bedroom and shut the door.

CHAPTER 5

*G*rayson pulled up to Harland Creek Farm and killed the engine. He noticed an unfamiliar car parked in the drive with Georgia tags.

He knew Elizabeth's children didn't live in Georgia.

He got out of his truck and took the steps two at a time to the front door.

He knocked on the door and a young woman opened the door.

She was in her early twenties, with long blond hair and blue eyes. She wore jeans that were a size too big and an oversized T-shirt.

"Can I help you?" She eyed him suspiciously and didn't invite him in.

"I'm here to see Ms. Elizabeth." He looked over her shoulder. It was easy enough to do since he towered over her.

"Can I ask who is calling?" She lifted her chin defiantly.

He chuckled. "No." He pushed past her and stepped inside the foyer.

"Excuse me. I didn't invite you in." She fisted her hands at her sides.

"Lady, I haven't been invited inside in years."

"I'll call the police." She glared at him.

"Good. The chief's name is Cooper. Tell him he owes me fifty dollars from our poker night." He stepped inside the living room.

"You have some nerve barging in here like you own the place." She got into his space and glared.

"Grayson, what's going on in here?" Elizabeth stepped into the living room using the aid of a walker.

He smiled. "Ms. Elizabeth. I'm just getting acquainted with your new..." He looked back at the young woman, unsure exactly who she was.

"Grayson McCade, this is Heather Smith. She's answered the ad in the paper for a caregiver. Someone to help until I get back on my feet."

"Sure you didn't advertise for a bodyguard?" He spoke under his breath so only Heather could hear.

Heather looked at Ms. Elizabeth. "You know him?"

"Yes, of course. Grayson has a farm next to mine. And his sister, Olivia, owns the florist shop in town. She buys a lot of my flowers and helps me ship to other florists they know in other parts of Mississippi." Ms. Elizabeth gave him a grateful smile.

"You're looking well, Ms. Elizabeth. You'll be dancing in no time." He smiled.

She barked out a laugh and swatted him on the arm. "You know I never dance."

He let his gaze slide over to Heather, who was watching him carefully.

"You got here just in time, Grayson. I was about to take Heather out to the flower fields so I could see what needs to be done."

"Perfect. I'll bring the four-wheeler around."

"I'm afraid I'm not going to be able to hop on that. At least

21

for a while. I was going to walk."

"Are you sure you want me to come, Ms. Elizabeth? I could stay here and clean up a bit while Grayson takes you down to the flowers."

He noticed Heather didn't bother looking at him. Who was this girl? And why did Elizabeth hire her so fast? He would have thought she would have chosen someone older, someone stronger.

Something about Heather didn't add up.

"I need you to go with me. Grayson won't be here every day. Just for picking up flowers. I need you so I can tell you what to do."

Heather's face fell.

Was she going to ransack the house while Elizabeth was out in the field?

Something told him to keep his eye on her.

"How are you managing the stairs?" Grayson asked.

"The doctor told me no stairs. But I'm tempted to climb them anyway. You know my sewing room is upstairs." She laughed and her eyes sparkled.

"Don't be going against the doctor's orders." He let her out the front door first. And then he held the door open for Heather.

She stepped outside but looked none too pleased at having to be in his company.

Too bad. He had a lot of respect for Ms. Elizabeth, and he wasn't going to just let some stranger try to rip her off.

"Why don't you hold on to me." Heather put one arm around Ms. Elizabeth's waist to assist her.

The older woman gave her a grateful smile.

"Here, let me help," Grayson offered.

"No, it's best if I can help her. That's why I am here." Heather scaled him with a look. "If you want to help, bring her walker outside."

He bristled but went inside to retrieve the walker.

"Thank you, Grayson, but Heather is right. She'll be here until I'm fully recovered so it's best for her to help when she can." She took the steps one at a time. Once they got to the bottom, she grabbed the walker with both hands.

They walked slowly to the fields. The dew was still on the ground and Grayson noticed that Heather kept her gaze averted. Even though Ms. Elizabeth was walking well with the walker, Heather hovered near her.

"I didn't know you planted so many tulips. And look how well they're doing. And I see your gladiolus is starting to come up for summer." Grayson stopped on the other side of the gate leading into the field of flowers.

"I just had to get the right conditions to have such a good crop of tulips. I'm pleased they turned out so well. I'll add more varieties in the fall." She pointed toward the field. "I had some requests from a few florists in Jackson and Memphis. Seems like gladiolus are going to be a big request for weddings. So I added more white and peach varieties along with the usual colors." Ms. Elizabeth looked on her field and smiled.

Grayson heard the soft inhale from Heather. He cut his eyes over in her direction.

She'd been so focused on watching the ground for anything that might trip Ms. Elizabeth that she'd not been looking at the fields.

Her mouth dropped and her eyes widened slightly. "You grew all these?"

Elizabeth nodded. "Sure did." The pride was evident in her voice. "Even when they said there was no way tulips would grow in Mississippi weather."

"I had no idea flowers grew like this. There are so many. Almost as far as the eye can see."

"You thought they grew them in a grocery store?" Grayson cocked his head.

She blinked and looked over at him. She remembered she obviously didn't think much of him and glared.

"I need to see what the roses are doing on the other end. I had Justin come water them, but he knows nothing about flowers."

"Who's Justin?" Heather asked.

"He is Grayson's farmhand." Elizabeth stopped at the fence.

"Justin knows cows, not flowers," Grayson added. "I'll get the four-wheeler and drive down there and report back. I'll take pictures for you with my phone."

"Wait." Ms. Elizabeth touched Heather on the arm. "Go with him."

"Me?" Heather cringed.

Not the usual reaction he got from a woman.

"Yes, you. I need you to go with him. Grayson will show you where the irrigation switch is and how to turn it on and off. He'll also tell you about the different flowers and how to inspect them."

"What about you?"

"I'll stay right here. If you're going to take care of me while I'm recovering, you're going to have to help me with the flowers. Unless you're not up for it…" Ms. Elizabeth cocked her head.

"Yes. I'm up for it," Heather said a little too quickly.

Grayson narrowed his eyes. He didn't trust the woman.

"Perfect. Now run along and I'll wait right here."

"I'll be right back with the four-wheeler." Grayson jogged back to the barn. When he pulled up to the older lady, he pulled the fold-up chair off the back of the four-wheeler.

"I thought you might like to sit in case it takes us a while." Grayson unfolded the chair and placed it by the fence.

"Thank you, Grayson." She gave him a weary smile.

"You ready?" Grayson turned to Heather.

"I am." She lifted her chin in a defiant stance.

He hopped on the four-wheeler and waited for her to get behind him.

Her gaze skittered from him to the small seat where she was expected to sit. She wiped her hands on her jeans and tried to get on behind him without actually touching him.

When she sat, she tried to sit as far back from him as possible.

He snorted. It was going to be a bumpy ride from where she was perched. But that was her problem, not his.

He started the engine and turned the handles in the direction into the field. He started slow as he drove through the large pathway and examined the multitude of colorful flowers.

He turned down the dirt path between the rows of gladiolus. Their spikey little heads were pushing through the soil.

He stopped and looked over his shoulder. "These are gladiolus."

"So they don't bloom in the spring." She pulled out a small notebook and pencil nub out of her jeans.

He frowned as she made a note. "They bloom in the summer. These are the white ones; these are pink and red, and those over there are peach. Farther down are the yellow and orange ones."

She nodded and scribbled a note.

"How often do I water them?"

"Depends on the forecast. We've been having a dry spell for a couple of weeks, so Justin has come over and turned on the irrigation system for Ms. Elizabeth."

"How long do I water for? And how will I know if when it rains it will be enough?" She tugged on her bottom lip.

"The irrigation system is on a timer. Ms. Elizabeth will

tell you if you need to water or not. All you do is turn the water on. I'll show you where that is when we finish looking at the flowers."

"That sounds easy enough." She made another note in her notebook.

"Let's go look at the roses." He gunned the engine and she jerked back and grabbed the back of his shirt to hold on.

She mumbled something under her breath, and he guessed it wasn't anything too nice.

"Sorry," he said over his shoulder. It had been a while since he'd ridden a four-wheeler with a passenger.

He turned down a different dirt row and stopped when he came to the first row of red roses.

He hopped off and stared at her.

"Well?" He didn't bother keeping the impatient tone out of his voice.

"Well, what?"

"You need to get off and inspect the roses. She's going to want a report when we get back. She's very concerned about her flowers. She doesn't need them to fail."

Heather scrambled off the four-wheeler and stood, her chin lifted.

He narrowed his eyes at her. She didn't look like any caregiver he'd ever seen.

"You don't look very old. I can't imagine you have had much experience on being a caregiver."

"I'm older than I look." She narrowed her eyes.

"And that would be?" He crossed his arms over his chest.

"I'm twenty-two." She matched his glare. "And how old are you?"

"I'm twenty-six. Thanks for asking. And how long have you been in this line of work?" He cocked his head.

"Mr. McCade, why are you so interested in my life? Don't you have enough to keep you busy with cows?"

He smirked. "Are you refusing to answer my question?"

"Less than a year. I've been a caretaker less than a year." She skated his question and walked down the long row of thorny rose bushes with no flowers. "There aren't any roses blooming. Is something wrong with them?" She scribbled on her pad.

"No. Roses won't bloom until summer."

"What about fertilizer? Is there any special care for roses?"

"Yes. But don't bother writing anything down. Ms. Elizabeth already has a printout taped to her kitchen door. She keeps a detailed schedule on watering, fertilizer, and harvesting."

"I see." She pressed her lips together and shoved the pad and pencil back in her jeans pocket.

Grayson walked behind her as she examined the flowers.

He ran his finger across a leaf. "The majority of the roses are red. She also has long-stemmed yellow and white and pink as well."

"It's April. So she didn't have any for Valentine's Day?" She frowned.

She was quick. He had to give her that.

"No. She's hoping to put in a greenhouse. That way she can grow throughout the year. Even when weather is bad. Come on, we need to check the tulips."

A smile tugged at the corner of her full lips.

Something stirred in his chest. He shook his head. She may be pretty but pretty wasn't always nice. He knew that from experience.

CHAPTER 6

*H*eather couldn't stop staring at all the tulips.

She'd never seen so much vibrant color in her life.

She'd always been surrounded by grays and blacks. Now she was standing in the midst of a rainbow.

"These will need to be harvested." Grayson propped his hands on his hips. "Everyone wants tulips as soon as spring arrives."

"Does your sister…"

"Olivia."

"Does Olivia sell all of these in her shop? Driving in, I noticed Harland Creek was a pretty small town."

"What it lacks in numbers, it makes up for in character."

She bristled at his response. She could read people. It was a trait that had gotten her through foster homes all her life.

It was perfectly clear to her. Grayson McCade didn't care for her.

He pulled out his cell phone. "The answer to your question is no."

"No, what?"

"No. My sister doesn't sell all of these tulips. But she has contacts in Jackson and Memphis that will." He sent a text.

"So how do I harvest?" She waited for an answer.

"*You* won't be doing anything." He turned on his booted heel. "You're here to take care of Elizabeth."

"I can do both. Take care of her and the farm." She struggled to keep up with his long stride. Her tennis shoe sank into a muddy spot and she had to stop long enough to pull it out.

He turned around and looked at her foot. "You're going to need to wear rubber boots when you are out here."

"I don't have any." She swallowed hard. She was doing so good until he showed up and began to point out how useless she was.

If he would just go and leave her alone to figure things out on her own.

He glared and headed back to the four-wheeler. By the time she reached him, he had already started the quad.

"And don't get your mud everywhere," he groused.

No sooner had she climbed on than he started off. She jerked backward and had to cling to him to set herself right.

They reached Elizabeth and she quickly climbed off.

"How are things looking?" Elizabeth was leaning against the gate.

"Good. The tulips need to be picked... er... harvested. If you can tell me how I can start on that right away."

Elizabeth grinned. "Easy, easy. First things first. Olivia will reach out to her contacts and figure out who needs what. Then we will reserve a cooler truck so we can have some place to hold them as well as transport them. That will take a couple of days."

"Do you usually harvest by yourself?" Heather glared at

Grayson who was leaning against the fence. She turned her attention to the field of brilliant colors.

"When I first started I did. But I had my children to help. After they married and moved away, I started hiring high school students. Now I can barely get someone who wants to do a hard day's labor." She shook her head. "The past couple of years I've had to rely on the kindness of my neighbors to lend a hand. I appreciate it but I don't want to be a burden."

"You are never a burden." Grayson shoved off the fence and gave her a gentle look. "At Harland Creek we are more than neighbors, we are family."

Elizabeth took his hands in hers and smiled. "Thanks for making an old woman feel good."

He shook his head and laughed.

Heather straightened. "Is there anything else that needs to be done for the flowers today?" She nodded toward Grayson and averted his gaze. "He said you have a schedule written down as to caring for the flowers."

"I do." Elizabeth looked up at the sky. "Since it looks like rain, there's no need to water today."

Heather looked up and frowned. "But the weather man said it's not going to rain."

"The weather man is always wrong." Elizabeth lifted her chin. "I stopped going by them years ago." She looked at Grayson. "What do you think, Grayson? Think it's going to rain?"

He lifted his face to the sky. "Probably get an evening shower."

Heather bristled. She wished Grayson would leave. She didn't need him here making her look bad in front of Elizabeth. She needed this job more than he realized.

Heather noticed how Elizabeth cringed when she turned toward the house.

"Why don't we go inside and you can rest. I can run to the grocery store and make you something to eat when I get back." Heather gently held Elizabeth's arm to support her.

"Thank you, Heather." Elizabeth gave her a grateful look. "You know where Mac's Grocery store is in town?"

"I don't think I passed it on my way in." She had gotten confused when she'd gotten on the town's square.

"I can take her." Grayson smiled wide.

Heather stopped in her tracks. Elizabeth turned and smiled. "That would be nice, Grayson. That way you can give her a tour of the town."

"But I won't have time today. I need to get groceries and get back here so you won't be alone." Heather swallowed.

"Oh, no worries, dear. Agnes is dropping by later this afternoon."

"Oh, I see." Heather tried to hide the disappointment in her voice.

After helping Elizabeth up the stairs to the front porch, she reached for the door handle. Elizabeth waved her hand.

"I think I want to sit out here for a while. It will soon be too hot to enjoy a day outside. Might as well enjoy it while I can." Elizabeth eased herself into a wicker rocking chair.

"I'll bring you the phone and something to drink."

"That's very thoughtful." Elizabeth rubbed her hip. "Did you get your list?"

Heather held it up. She tossed her backpack on her shoulder.

"Grab my purse and I'll give you a blank check for the groceries."

Heather ducked inside and grabbed Elizabeth's purse off the kitchen counter. She stepped out onto the porch and handed it to the woman. Elizabeth dug around in her purse and pulled out her checkbook and pen. She quickly signed her name and handed the check to Heather. "Don't forget to pick up whatever food you want or think we need."

"Okay." She folded the paper and stuck it in her backpack. "I'll hurry back."

"No need." Elizabeth smiled. "Enjoy your time away from the farm. It might be your last for a while."

CHAPTER 7

*G*rayson eyed Heather as she clutched her worn backpack to her chest. "You can put that in the back seat, you know."

"No, thank you." She turned her attention out the truck window as they drove into town. "How far is the grocery store?"

"A few blocks off the square." He cast a glance at her before turning onto the square. He noticed she reached over for the passenger grab handle.

"Any trouble making it around the square?" He arched his brow.

"There needs to be more signs." She scowled. "How do people know who gets to go and who has to yield?"

"To be fair, we had a yield sign up, but it got knocked down at the Christmas parade. A combine carrying Santa Claus hit it."

"What's a combine?" She looked at him and blinked.

"Are you serious? I thought you were raised in the South. How do you not know what a combine is?"

33

Her full lips tightened into a thin line and she looked away.

A twinge of guilt hit him in the chest. "A combine is a large tractor. Usually used for harvesting crops."

After a few tense seconds she looked straight ahead. "I was born in Georgia but lived in Atlanta all my life. Never really been in the country."

"So your family is from Atlanta?"

"I have no family." She glanced over at him. "I was an only child. My parents are gone. It's just me." She glanced away.

"What about…"

"Is that your sister's flower shop? Roses and Lace Flower Shop?" She pointed at the pink-and-white-painted building next to the hair salon. Olivia was standing on the sidewalk arguing with Markus who worked for the electric company. Sylvia and Maggie, stylists at the S&M beauty salon, had flanked Olivia and were pointing fingers at the poor lineman.

"Yes. And it looks like she needs some help."

"I don't know about that. I feel sorry for the lineman," she muttered.

He pulled the truck into an empty parking lot in front of the shop. He cut the engine and slid out of the truck.

"What's going on?" He looked at Olivia who had gone white.

"The electricity is out." She looked at him with wide panicked eyes.

"Grayson, tell Markus we need electricity at the salon." Sylvia glared.

"My flowers. What about my flowers?" Olivia's eyes darted from him back to her shop.

"I'm sorry, ladies. I'm trying to get it on as fast as I can. The guys on the other end of town are working on it. Seems like a squirrel is the culprit." Markus shrugged.

"Grayson." Olivia grabbed his hand and looked like she was going to faint.

"It's okay. He's working on it. Aren't you, Markus?"

"I'm doing the best I can on my end. The holdup is the other guys."

"Sylvia, Maggie. Go on back to your shop. Tell your clients the situation. I'm sure they'll understand. I'll be over there in a minute."

Sylvia and Maggie reluctantly went back to the salon, none too pleased.

"As long as you keep the cooler door shut, the flowers should be okay," Grayson assured her.

"Are you sure?"

"I'm sure." He nodded. "Let me go get Sylvia and Maggie settled and I'll be back." He jogged over to the salon.

CHAPTER 8

"*W*ait. I've got five arrangements I have to make and deliver today. I need to get into the cooler to the flowers. I can't just keep the door shut." Olivia sighed.

"What if you make the arrangements inside the cooler? And then take them all out at once? Would that work?" Heather offered.

Olivia blinked. "Actually, that might. I'll have to move all the stuff I need inside."

"I'll help. That way you won't have to keep the door open long."

"Thank you." Olivia held her hand out. "You must think I'm terribly rude. My name is Olivia McCade."

"I know. Grayson told me." Heather stuck out her hand. "I'm Heather Smith. I'm Ms. Elizabeth Harland's caretaker. I'm here while she's recovering from hip surgery."

Olivia smiled wide. "I'm so glad to meet you, Heather. Come inside. So how did you meet Grayson?"

Heather glanced over at the salon. "He came over to the

farm. Your brother is supposed to be taking me to the grocery store since I don't know the town very well."

"How generous of him." Olivia grinned and held the door open. "Come on inside."

Heather stepped inside. The sweet scent of flowers washed over her. She looked at the wall of balloons and stand of greeting cards along one side of the room. There was a tall shelf with artificial arrangements of varying sizes and flowers. She even had some live potted plants.

Olivia didn't stop moving as she grabbed a stack of order forms. She headed over to the wall of vases behind the counter and began to gather supplies.

"Need some help?" Heather asked.

"That would be great." Olivia gave her a brilliant smile. "My assistant, Amy, had a dental appointment and she didn't have time to go over today's orders." She held out the orders to Heather. "If you can read out the name and what the flowers are for, I'll gather everything. First, let me grab a cart." She went in the back room and returned pushing a cart. "I'm ready."

Heather glanced down at the first order. "This first one is for Lois Garfield. To be delivered at the hospital. From Agnes. There's no last name."

"That's okay. We only have one Agnes in Harland Creek." Olivia smiled.

"She the one with the funny hat?"

"Yes! You already met her?"

"Yes, at Ms. Elizabeth's." Heather looked back at the order. "She wants to send a flower arrangement to the hospital for Lois. Card needs to read 'Get well soon or we'll replace you at Bunko.' Heather snorted. "It also says she doesn't want to send anything too fancy." Heather looked at Olivia.

"Ah, she wants an arrangement of pansies with a get well

soon balloon." Olivia quickly gathered the vase, green stuff for the vase, and a yellow polka-dot bow. She put them on the rolling cart and turned back to Heather. "Next order."

Heather held up the next order slip. "This is for Emily Douglas. Also delivered to the hospital. This is from her Sunday school class, congratulating her and her husband on their new baby, Lilliana. They want something nice under seventy-five dollars."

"They want pink and white tulips and a pink bear with balloons." Olivia gathered her supplies. "Okay, next order."

"This goes to Mildred Agnew. Her son Michael wants to send her six roses. Card reads, "Happy Birthday to the best mom in the world." Suddenly Heather felt very out of place.

"That was easy enough." Olivia gathered the supplies.

"Next."

"This is for Samantha Williams at her work. Happy Anniversary. There's a note that says do something different than the usual roses." Heather looked at Olivia.

Oliva tapped her finger to her lips and looked at the cooler of flowers. "That's Amy's mother. I know. White roses, carnations, and blue alstroemeria, blue delphinium, baby's breath, seeded eucalyptus, and assorted greenery."

"Wow, you're good. I don't even know what those flowers look like, but it sounds pretty." Heather arched her eyebrow.

Olivia laughed.

The bell above the door tinkled as Grayson walked in. "What's going on?"

"Heather is helping me gather my supplies so I can take them in the cooler and make the arrangements in there."

"That's a brilliant idea, Olivia." Grayson nodded.

"It wasn't me. It was Heather's idea."

Heather noticed the change in Grayson's demeanor. She looked away and back at the last order.

"So this last one goes to the school. It's for Julia Brooks. I think it's from her parents." Heather squinted. "But the card is supposed to read Secret Admirer. And it says price is no limit."

"Julia is going through an awkward phase. While her friends are all getting boyfriends, she is not. And her parents are trying to make her feel better. Give her a boost of confidence." Olivia gave her a sad smile.

"I see." Heather could sympathize.

"What would you want in a flower arrangement?" Olivia asked her.

"Me?" She pointed to herself.

"Yes, you. What were your most favorite flowers you've ever received?" Olivia's eyes sparkled.

Heather shook her head. "I wouldn't know. I've never gotten flowers."

Olivia froze. "Never?"

Heather shook her head, uncomfortable with the change in conversation. She cleared her throat. "What would you want? You did so well with picking out the right flowers for everyone else. Do Julia's."

Olivia cocked her head and thought for a second. "I would do tulips and irises. In every shade of the rainbow."

"And the bow?" Heather grinned.

"A simple white bow so it doesn't overwhelm the bouquet." Olivia gathered her supplies and added them to the rolling cart.

"Do you have someone to deliver these? Where's Amy?" Grayson scowled.

"Dentist appointment. I think Sam said something about dropping by. He offered to help so you can tend to your cows. But I see you got distracted." Olivia grinned and cut her eyes at Heather.

"I really should get to the grocery store." Heather shifted her weight.

"Yeah, she needs to get back to Ms. Elizabeth." Grayson pushed the cart into the walk-in cooler where the flowers were. When he came out, he propped his hands on his hips. "Markus said the electricity shouldn't be out too much longer. Want me to turn the Closed sign so no one will come in?"

"Yes. Thanks." She gave a sad smile. "Nobody could buy anything anyway. The credit card machine is electric."

"Nice meeting you." Heather gave her a little wave and headed for the door.

"Wait!" Olivia ran to the back room and reappeared with a small bouquet of white daisies wrapped with a bow. "Here. For all your help."

"I can't take those." Heather shook her head.

"Of course you can. They're a gift." Olivia held them out.

Heather took the bouquet in her hands and lifted them to her nose. They smelled delicate and light, not at all over-whelming.

"Thank you." She smiled.

"Now you've gotten flowers." Olivia nodded and headed into the back room.

Heather could feel Grayson's stare. She chose to ignore him. Lifting her chin and gripping the tiny bouquet in her hand, she walked out the door.

CHAPTER 9

*T*hey drove in silence to the grocery store. Once they got to Mac's Grocery, Heather looked unsure what to do with her bouquet.

"You can leave them in the truck. I'll crack a window. It's not hot enough for them to droop."

She frowned. "I need to put them in water."

"Hang on." He got out of the truck and went around to the bed of his truck. He opened the tailgate, then opened the cooler he kept in the back there and pulled out a water.

He walked around to her side of the truck and opened her door. Unscrewing the bottle of water, he handed it to her. "Pour some out and then put it in the cupholder and keep the bouquet in it."

"Thanks," she said quietly before taking the bottle of water. She took a drink before putting her flowers inside the opening.

"I have another bottle if you're thirsty."

"No, thank you. Just don't like to waste." She got out and shut the door behind her. She headed for the entrance to Mac's.

He quickly caught up.

"So what's on your list?" He craned his neck to look at the piece of paper she was holding.

"You know, you can go back and help your sister and just pick me up when I'm done." She stopped and looked at him.

"She said Sam was coming to help. Besides, I promised Ms. Elizabeth to give you a tour of our town. I wouldn't be a good neighbor if I didn't do that."

"You could go look at your cows, or whatever you do with them." She cringed.

"I *looked* at them this morning." He snorted. "I'll *look* at them when I get home."

She glared. "You're making fun of me."

"Teasing you. And you are an easy target. Just trying to figure you out," he countered.

"Don't bother." She turned on her heel and headed inside the store.

He fought back a grin.

"Good afternoon," Mac greeted them.

"Hi, Mac," Grayson greeted the older man wearing khakis and a short-sleeve white shirt.

"Who's your friend, Grayson?" Mac smiled at Heather.

"This is Heather Smith. She is the caretaker for Ms. Elizabeth while she gets back on her feet."

"Nice to meet you, Heather. I'm Mac Conners. The owner of the grocery. How is Ms. Elizabeth doing? We sure do miss her at church."

"She's doing okay." Heather hesitated. "I'm not sure how long she'll be needing my help."

"I see you have your list. Let me know if you need any help." Mac gave her a generous smile before heading over to help the cashier who needed change.

She grabbed a shopping cart.

"Here, I'll push while you shop." Grayson didn't wait for

her to respond but nudged her out of the way and turned the cart down the first aisles.

She pressed her lips into a thin line and studied the sheet.

"What do you need?"

"Apples and bananas." She rushed ahead of him to the produce. She inspected and chose the best apples before bagging them.

He began to pick up a group of bananas, but she shook her head. "No, not those."

"Why? What's wrong with them?"

"They're too ripe. They won't last long." She grabbed some bananas that looked almost green.

After she placed them in the cart, she glanced over at the oranges.

"Mac gets those in fresh from Florida. Best oranges I've ever eaten." Grayson pushed the cart by the stand of oranges.

She glanced at the list and then back at the oranges.

"You'll won't find any better," he said again.

She went to the oranges and carefully chose three and placed them in a bag. She pulled out a pencil and scribbled something on the paper.

She didn't say much when they went through the store. He watched as she carefully examined and compared prices. She looked unsure when she stopped at the meat section.

He glanced at his watch. He needed to get back to his farm.

He stepped up beside her and pointed to a package of ground beef. "I recommend this beef."

"But it's higher than the other." She pointed to a different container.

"I know. The other is discounted because it's older meat. You don't want that. Besides, Ms. Elizabeth likes to use the freshest ingredients when she can."

Heather hesitated for a moment and then grabbed the package he suggested.

"Anything else on your list?"

She glanced down. Her cheeks burned. "I need to get some peanut butter."

"Aisle three."

She hurried ahead of him and picked the cheapest brand of peanut butter the grocery store carried.

"Just get the name brand." Grayson frowned.

"No, this is fine." She stuck it in the cart and headed toward the cashier before he could get her to change her mind.

"Hi, Irene." Grayson smiled at the older woman checking them out. "How are you?"

"I'm still alive. So that's something." She cut her eyes at Heather. "Who's your friend, Grayson."

"This is Heather Smith. She's Ms. Elizabeth's caretaker."

Irene burst out laughing. "You best not be saying that around Elizabeth. She hates being reminded she's getting old. Like me." Irene continued to ring up the groceries. "How are you liking it in Harland Creek? Young thing like you is probably bored to death."

"Oh no. It's a very pretty town. And most everyone has been friendly." Heather gave him serious side-eye.

He cringed. Maybe he hadn't exactly rolled out the welcome mat with her, but he had known women like her in the past. Young, pretty, with a yearning to move on to the next best thing.

"Good. We like to have a good report of our town. We may be small, but we are like family." Irene nodded. "That will be ninety-five dollars."

Heather pulled out the check that Elizabeth had given her. She filled it in and handed the check to Irene.

"Normally we need to see ID if a stranger is giving a

check. But since this is Elizabeth's and Grayson can vouch for you, I'll make an exception." Irene smiled.

"Thank you." Heather seemed to relax a little and took the receipt that Irene held out.

Irene pulled a lollipop out of a jar next to the register. "Here you go. Welcome to Harland Creek."

Heather's face seem to light up with the simple gift. It wasn't excitement he saw. To Grayson it looked like hope.

CHAPTER 10

*T*he ride back had been strained. Heather didn't want to talk to Grayson or answer any of his nosy questions. Thankfully, Justin had called about a problem with one of his cows. By the time he'd gotten off the phone, they were pulling into Elizabeth's driveway.

"Thank you for the ride. I know the town a little better now, so I can get around with no problem." She gave him a tight smile and slid out of the truck.

"I'll help with the groceries." He killed the engine and opened the back door of the truck.

"I can…"

"Heather. I'll help. You can't take all these groceries in at one time. Besides, this way is quicker. I've got to get back to the farm." He grabbed multiple bags in both hands, leaving her with just the one bag with the oranges.

She grabbed the milk and her flowers, and slammed the door.

"That was quick." Elizabeth opened the screen door and let them in. "I expected you two to be gone for a few hours."

"She was eager to get back."

Heather scowled as he set the bags of groceries on the kitchen counter.

"Grayson, would you like something to drink?" Elizabeth offered.

"No, ma'am. I've got to be going." He looked at Heather. "You forgot your flowers."

"Flowers? That wasn't on the list." Elizabeth frowned.

"I didn't buy them." Heather cleared her throat. "They were a gift from Olivia."

"How nice." Elizabeth smiled. "Olivia's a sweet girl." She opened a cabinet. "I have just the vase for it." She pulled down a cut glass vase and filled it with water.

She took the bouquet of flowers and placed them inside the vase. She rearranged until it met her satisfaction. "There. Now you can place this beside your bed. There is nothing like waking up to fresh flowers."

Elizabeth followed Grayson out to the front porch while Heather quickly put away the groceries. She peered around the doorway. They were talking on the front porch. She opened her backpack and stuffed the oranges and jar of peanut butter inside. She zipped it and began putting away the groceries.

By the time Elizabeth walked inside she was done.

"Did you find everything on the list?" Elizabeth eased into a kitchen chair.

"I did." She rubbed her hands on her jeans. She spotted the kitchen kettle on the stove. "Would you like a cup of tea?"

"You up for making it?" Elizabeth eyed her.

"Sure. How hard could a cup of tea be?" She busied herself and turned the stove on and grabbed two mugs out of the cabinet.

"Come sit." Elizabeth patted the chair next to her.

Heather eased into the chair. She dug around in her backpack and pulled out her notebook and pencil.

Elizabeth laughed. "You won't need that. I just want to ask you something."

She shifted in her seat. "About?"

"I need you to tell me the truth." Elizabeth gave her a stern look.

She nodded, her throat too dry to speak. She'd only made it a day before her secret came out.

She'd made a promise she had intended to keep. She failed.

"I figured cooking wasn't your specialty." Elizabeth arched her brow.

She blinked.

"Don't lie. I watched you last night."

"What gave me away?" Relief slid through her like a cool spring rain.

"You wrote down every ingredient that went into each dish" Elizabeth said. "Plus, you didn't know what a table-spoon was." She grinned.

"Sorry. I should have told you. But I'm a fast learner." The kettle began to whistle. Heather stood and turned off the heat. She put two tea bags into each cup and poured the hot water over them. She placed one mug in front of Elizabeth.

She sat down and wrapped her hands around her hot mug of tea but couldn't bring herself to look at Elizabeth. Would she fire her because she found her lacking?

"Your mother didn't teach you how to cook?"

Heather swallowed. "No. She wasn't around." It wasn't a lie, but it wasn't exactly the truth either.

"I see." Elizabeth nodded slowly. "Go look in the large cabinet in the living room. The one with all my quilts. There should be a notebook. Bring it in here."

"But I have a notebook." Heather's fingers brushed against her backpack.

"You need a new one." Elizabeth shook her head.

Heather walked into the living room and opened the dark doors of the cabinet. She was greeted with cheery quilts sewn with brilliant-colored fabrics. There had to be at least thirty quilts stashed in here.

She ran her fingers across the different quilt patterns.

"Did you find it?" Elizabeth called out from the kitchen.

"Sorry. I was looking at your quilts. Did you make all these?"

"I did. Look in the drawer at the bottom. There should be a notebook with flowers on it."

Heather knelt and opened the drawer. She moved some random papers around until she spotted a dark-pink notebook with blue flowers on it.

Standing, she shut the cabinet drawers and walked into the kitchen.

"Is this the one?" She held it up.

"Yes." Elizabeth smiled and took a sip of her tea.

Heather sat and placed the notebook in front of the older woman.

Elizabeth's weathered hand slowly pushed it in front of Heather. "This is for you. "

"Me?"

"Yes. This is going to be your recipe book. Every woman needs to know how to cook." Elizabeth nodded firmly.

"To be able to catch a man?" Heather snorted. "That's the last thing on my mind."

"Who said anything about a man? Every woman needs to know how to cook for herself. If you get the hankering for a pot roast on Saturday afternoon, don't you want to know how to make it?"

Just the idea made her mouth water. She nodded.

"And fried chicken with mashed potatoes and gravy on Sunday?"

"You still cook like that for yourself?"

"Of course I do. I'm not going to sit around and gnaw on some peanut butter sandwiches just because I'm old. Eating well is a sign of self-respect." Elizabeth tapped her finger on the floral notebook. "I want you to write down recipes we make in here. That way you'll know how to make them yourself. No matter where you are." Elizabeth took a sip of her tea. "Speaking of which, do you know where you'll go after I'm healed?"

The thought made Heather terribly sad.

"I haven't decided."

"I suppose you'll be heading for greener pastures. You young people like the city."

"I've had enough city to last me a lifetime," Heather said softly.

Elizabeth seemed to be studying her.

Heather shrugged. "I'm not sure what I'll do after this. Right now, I'm focused on today and helping you get better. I saw a sheet of exercises the physical therapist wants you to do." She flipped through some papers scattered on the kitchen table. She found the sheet.

"But first." Elizabeth held her hand up. "Let's make lunch. Then we can exercise and see about the flowers. I think we should make a pasta salad with these fresh vegetables Agnes brought. Be sure to write down the recipe as we go. You'll want to make it again. That I promise."

"Sounds like a plan." Heather smiled.

CHAPTER 11

*H*eather quickly settled into a routine around the farm. She would get up early and get the coffee ready before Elizabeth came into the kitchen. Whenever Elizabeth would plan out a meal, she would get Heather to write down exactly how it was made in her new floral notebook. Each night before bed, Heather would give her flowers fresh water and reread all the recipes she'd gathered.

To some it might seem like a small inconsequential thing. To her it was like she was gathering treasures to last a lifetime.

"Good morning." Elizabeth hobbled into the kitchen.

"Good morning. I thought I'd make some eggs and bacon for breakfast this morning." Heather handed her a cup of coffee.

"Not today. We don't have time for that today." Elizabeth sat down. "Toast and jam will have to do."

Heather studied the calendar on the wall by the refrigerator. "I don't see any appointments for today. And we turned on the irrigation for the flowers yesterday."

"We have a different kind of appointment." She sipped her coffee. "It's Sunday. We have church today."

Heather's stomach sunk. That was the last place she wanted to go.

"Are you sure you feel up to it?" She opened the pantry door and pulled out the bread.

"If I'm up for cooking and looking after the farm, then I'm up for church." Elizabeth sipped her coffee.

Heather sighed. She stuck two pieces of bread into the toaster and pushed the button down.

"The thing is… I don't have anything to wear for church." She clasped her hands in front of her.

"You don't need anything fancy. You don't need a dress or anything."

She cringed and eased into the seat next to Elizabeth. "What I mean is, all I have are jeans and T-shirts. I don't have anything suitable for church."

"Jeans are fine. It's a small church. Not fancy." Elizabeth cocked her head. "Although I am surprised. A pretty young woman like you ought to have a nice blouse or shirt. For going out."

"I'm more of a homebody." She ducked her head.

Elizabeth grinned. "That's okay. I think Maggie has some clothes in the closet from before she got married. I don't even know if they are in style or not. I'm not much up on the latest fashion."

"Oh, I don't know." It had been a while since she'd been to church. One of her foster parents had taken her a few times. But the priest was stern and said a lot of big words she didn't understand. Plus, all the statues gave her the creeps.

The toaster popped the toasted bread up. Heather stood and gathered the jam and put the toast on plates. She pulled out some strawberries from the refrigerator and put them in a pretty cut glass bowl. She placed the fruit and toast on the table. She refilled the coffee cups before sitting down.

"Thank you, Heather. This looks really good." Elizabeth stirred her coffee. "We'll eat and then get ready for church. We can go in my truck so we won't use up your gas."

"The truck? Are you sure you can manage it? It seems pretty high." Heather frowned.

"I have a small footstool in the kitchen closet. I'll use that. I need to get used to using my own truck. It's not like you'll be here forever." Elizabeth placed a swatch of blackberry jam on her toast.

Heather's heart sunk a little. Those weren't the words she wanted to hear. She needed to keep this job for as long as she could. She also knew she needed to be lining up her next job. Maybe church was the place she could do that.

As nervous as she was about attending, she knew it would give her the best opportunity to meet as many possible people she could work for after her job with Elizabeth was over.

Who knows, maybe she might find a lead on her next job.

Grabbing a piece of toast, she smiled to herself and smoothed a thick layer of jam.

CHAPTER 12

"*I* can't go. I changed my mind." Heather's hands gripped the steering wheel tightly.

"I told you no one is going to care that you're not wearing a dress."

"But they will be caring that I'm wearing a paisley vest that's two sizes too small." She looked down at her nineties attire. She'd worn her best jeans, but Elizabeth had talked her into wearing a white puffy-sleeved shirt and pink and green paisley vest of her daughter's to dress it up a bit. She'd even let Elizabeth talk her into wearing some platform sandals she pulled out of the back of the closet. She'd been too horrified at the vest to notice how bad the shoes really were.

"God doesn't look at outward appearances. He looks at the heart."

"Oh, I think He's going to make an exception today. Besides, everyone is going to be looking at this hot mess." She looked down at herself, horrified. "Now I know why Maggie left these behind," she muttered.

"Elizabeth!" Agnes waved from her perch at the top step of the little white church.

"Let's go before someone takes my seat." Elizabeth opened the door and tried to get out.

"Wait! Before you fall." Heather hurried out of the truck. She got to Elizabeth before she stepped out of the truck. "Let me get the stool." She retrieved the stool from the back seat and set it down in front of Elizabeth's door.

"I think it will be easier going down than trying to get me up." Elizabeth snorted.

Heather supported her by the arm as she slowly climbed down.

Elizabeth sighed loudly.

"Well, you're getting around better." Agnes smiled at her friend. She looked over at Heather and frowned. "Who dressed you, honey?" She cut her eyes at Elizabeth.

Her shoulders slumped.

"What's with you two? I'm going to tell you like I told her. Outward appearances don't matter to God…"

"In this case it does." Agnes grimaced. "I haven't seen fashion that bad since… well, the late eighties."

"Ugh." Heather buried her face in her hands. "I can't walk inside like this."

"Agnes, since when did you become such a fashionista?" Elizabeth scowled.

"Since my niece became a supermodel." Agnes shrugged. "I try to keep up with the latest fashion." She pointed a finger in Heather's direction. "And that ain't it."

"Is that a paisley vest? I haven't seen one of those since eighth grade." A middle-aged woman cocked her head.

"Heather, this is Jana Giles. She's the Sunday school teacher for young married couples. Jana, this is Heather Smith. She is here taking care of me while I recover from hip surgery."

"Nice to meet you, Heather. Glad you are here taking such good care of Elizabeth. Walk in with me, Elizabeth. I need to ask you some questions about what I'm doing wrong with my hyacinths. Those suckers just won't bloom for me." Jana frowned.

"We'll be along shortly." Agnes gripped Heather's arm. "I need to discuss something with Heather."

When they were out of reach, Agnes tugged her toward her car.

"What did you want to talk about?" Heather looked around.

"Honey, Elizabeth is my best friend. But that woman has no fashion. I'm surprised you allowed her to talk you into wearing this." She shook her head and opened the trunk of her car.

"It's my fault. The only clothes I have are jeans and T-shirts. I told her I didn't have any dressy clothes. She found these in the closet from her daughter."

"Good Lord, child. Her daughter is in her forties. No one is wearing paisley vests with puffy-sleeved shirts." Agnes shook her head. "I know you don't want to upset Elizabeth and you are trying to do a good job. But that doesn't mean you can't voice your own opinion. Stand up for yourself." Agnes looked back in the trunk and opened a box. She smiled.

"What's this?"

"My niece sent me these when I asked her for donations for a silent auction we have coming up in the fall. They are designer clothes that have only been worn once." Agnes pulled out a sparkly black top.

"I think that might be too dressy." Heather touched the sleeve of the silky material.

"Help me dig around until we find something."

They dug around, checking out each item.

"I think this will do." Agnes held out a mocha-colored lace top. "You can wear this with your jeans. Plus, it will draw attention away from your shoes." She gave her a cheery smile.

Heather took it.

"Get in the back seat of my car and change your shirt. I'm always parked on the other end of the parking lot. No one will see you here."

"Are you sure?" Heather looked around. Everyone was filing into the church like ants. No one was milling around the parking lot.

"Yes. Now hurry. I'll be inside." Agnes grabbed her vest and shoved it in the back of the box.

"Hey, I have to give that back to Elizabeth." Heather gave her a wide-eyed look.

"No, you're not. I'm burning it. She won't miss it. Now get changed." Agnes shut the trunk and marched toward the white building.

Heather groaned and slid into the back seat of the older model car. She shut the door behind her. It smelled of an odd combination of honey and mothballs. She took one more glance and quickly took off the puffy shirt and tossed it on the floor. She slid the lacey shirt on and quickly buttoned it up.

"What are you doing?"

She froze at the familiar male voice. Clenching the shirt together, she jerked her head to the right. Grayson was bent down, peering inside.

"Jerk," she muttered and turned her back on him and stepped out of the car. "Do you make it a habit to spy on women? You know there is a law against watching women undress."

His eyebrows shot up. "You were undressing?"

"No, you idiot. I was getting dressed." She blinked. The words didn't sound any less innocent.

He stared at her.

"I was changing my shirt, if you have to know."

"Why were you changing your shirt?" He crossed his arms over his chest and stared at her hard, like he didn't believe her.

She opened the door to the back seat and pulled out the puffy shirt. "Because Elizabeth gave me this shirt to wear."

He frowned.

"It was her daughter's. From twenty years ago. Agnes took pity on me and gave me a shirt her niece sent for a silent auction." She lifted her chin, daring him to challenge her.

"Why did Elizabeth give you clothes?" He narrowed his eyes and threw the shirt into the back seat of the car.

"Because all I have are T-shirts and jeans. I may not have been in a lot of churches, but I know how they work. People judge you when you don't have nice clothes."

His gaze drifted down the front of her.

"Is there anything else or do I have your permission to go inside?" She crossed her arms over her chest.

He held up his hands in a defensive gesture and took a step back.

She tried to storm away but her platform heel went sideways on the gravel of the church parking lot. She felt herself falling.

Suddenly large hands were around her waist, and she found herself pressed into a hard chest.

"You okay?" He looked down at her with those hard blue eyes.

Her breath hitched in her throat. She put her hands flat against his chest and pushed him away.

"I'm fine. Thank you." Her words were low.

"Nice shoes."

She cringed as she opened the door and headed inside.

CHAPTER 13

*G*rayson tried to ignore the twist of guilt in his gut.

He hadn't meant to hurt Heather's feelings. He just wanted to make sure she wasn't trying to steal anything from Agnes' car. Harland Creek was a small town and crime was a rare thing. He just wanted it to stay that way.

When he saw the ugly shirt and shoes that looked like something his mom had worn, he knew she had been telling the truth. What he wanted to know was, why didn't a woman as beautiful as Heather not own any decent clothes?

He followed her into the church at a safe distance.

She quickly found Elizabeth in the front row and sat just as the choir started singing.

"Hey, man. Didn't think you were going to make it on time." Sam stood and slapped him on the back.

Grayson slid into the pew between him and Olivia. "Yeah. I was just getting to know the new girl."

Sam snorted. "I bet you were."

"That's not what I mean." Grayson glared.

Sam held his hands up. "I'm not judging. I think it's great

you are getting back out there in the dating pond. It's time you moved on."

"I moved on a while ago." Grayson glanced over at the Fran Gleason's son sitting next to him to check out the page number. He flipped the hymnal to the correct page. He tried singing the hymn, but he couldn't stop looking at Heather and studying her every move.

She opened the hymn book only after Elizabeth handed her one. She didn't sing along, and he wondered if she even knew the words. He was not the only one who was curious about the new girl.

After the pastor stepped up to the pulpit, everyone quieted.

Sloan Jackson and his sister Allison were studying Heather. As a policeman, Sloan would want to know about the stranger in town. Knowing Allison, she'd probably want to bake her a casserole, if she had the time. She'd been busy lining up jobs as an interior decorator in Harland Creek.

Sitting next to Sloan was his best friend, Mitch Woods. He wasn't as close to Mitch as he was Sloan. As a contractor, Mitch ran in the same circles as Sam. Sam preferred new construction while Mitch was content with remodeling jobs.

Grayson frowned. Mitch was single and good-looking. And he couldn't stop looking at Heather.

"If you hold that hymnal any tighter, you are going to tear it in half," Sam whispered.

Grayson looked at his white-knuckled grip on the book. He shut the book and glared at his friend.

"What's wrong with you? You're acting so grumpy. Did you not eat before you got here? Are you hangry?" Sam arched his eyebrow.

Gertrude Matthews turned around and glared at both of them. "If you two don't keep it down, I'm going to slap you into next week." She turned to face the front of the church and gave them her gray bun.

Sam snorted and lowered his voice. "I haven't been reprimanded in church since I was ten."

Grayson felt a smile tug at his mouth. He pressed his lips into a thin line.

Grayson couldn't keep his mind focused on the sermon. Instead, he found his thoughts on Heather.

CHAPTER 14

*H*eather's stomach growled as they drove back to Elizabeth's house. She put her hand over it to keep it from being so loud. "What do you feel like for lunch?" She glanced over at Elizabeth.

"We could make some fried chicken and mashed potatoes. I'll even show you how to make biscuits." Elizabeth nodded.

"But won't that take hours?" She didn't know if she wanted to wait that long. "We could do some sandwiches."

"Not on Sunday. Besides, if you're going to do something right, it takes time." Elizabeth nodded.

Anxiety tingled at the base of Heather's spine. She had eaten her oranges that she'd kept in her room. But she still had peanut butter, she reminded herself.

"How did you like church?"

"It was fine. People seemed… friendly."

Elizabeth laughed out loud. "You mean nosy. I saw how everyone surrounded you and kept asking you questions." She shrugged. "In a small town, anytime someone new moves in, people are naturally curious."

"Apparently," Heather muttered and turned into the

driveway leading to the house.

"I noticed Agnes gave you a different shirt." Elizabeth nodded.

"Yeah, sorry. It's just…"

Elizabeth held up her hand. "No need to apologize. I may know flowers, but I have no idea about what young women wear these days. Back when I was growing up, it didn't matter what you wore as long as it covered you up." She nodded finally.

Heather snorted.

Elizabeth gave her look.

She pulled up close to the house and got out. She got the step stool out of the back and positioned it in front of Elizabeth's door.

"I think we got this system down pat," Elizabeth said as she made her way down. "Now, let's get inside and change into something more comfortable. Then we'll get to cooking. Make sure you get your recipe notebook and write down every step. You'll want this meal in your arsenal when you have a family of your own." Elizabeth smiled and slowly made her way inside.

Heather climbed the stairs to her room. She stood in front of the mirror hanging on the door.

A family of your own.

Is that something she would ever have?

She shook her head and forced those thoughts away.

Right now, she needed to make sure she was accepted into Harland Creek before she thought beyond that.

She quickly changed into her jeans and T-shirt and sneakers. She opened her jar of peanut butter and scooped a small spoonful and ate it.

That would tide her over until the chicken was done.

Grabbing her floral notebook, she bounded down the stairs.

CHAPTER 15

*H*eather bolted up in bed at the sound of her alarm clock. She reached for her phone and shut off the annoying buzzer. She was used to jerking away at any slight noise. But since she'd been at Elizabeth's, the sound of birds and croaking of frogs soon lulled her to sleep instead of keeping her awake.

She crawled out of bed and found her sweatpants on the floor. She slipped them on under her T-shirt. She pulled the drawstring tight to keep the pants from falling, then bent down and rolled up both pant legs.

She glanced over at the shirt draped carefully over the back of the chair. She'd never worn anything as nice as the shirt Agnes let her borrow. She was thankful to the older woman. She might have felt out of place in the church yesterday, but at least she hadn't looked out of place.

After the service, Olivia had come over and introduced a beautiful blond woman named Allison. Allison had complimented her on her shirt and welcomed her to the town. She was also introduced to the preacher and his wife, although she had forgotten their names. She'd been so nervous to get back to the farm that the majority of the names eluded her.

The only reason she remembered Allison and Olivia's names is they seemed to be around her age and they'd been really nice to her.

Grayson had even come up and introduced Mitch to her. Mitch was completely different than Grayson. While both men were handsome, Mitch was warm and friendly and didn't press her too much with personal questions. Unlike Grayson who put his nose into other people's business.

She didn't mind as long as he kept it out of her business.

She hurried downstairs and started the coffee pot. While she sat at the kitchen table, she made some notes.

Today they would be harvesting flowers and putting them in a refrigerated truck that was arriving from Memphis. A company from Tennessee would be delivering them to various florists within the state. According to Elizabeth, they could only harvest in the mornings or evenings to keep the flowers at their freshest. Elizabeth had numerous large buckets in the barn they would use to keep the cut flowers in water.

She'd gone over her notes on how to cut the flower at a forty-five-degree angle and to remove any extra leaves below the water line.

Heather stood and grabbed two mugs out of the cabinet and poured herself a cup. She glanced at the clock on the wall. It wasn't even five thirty yet.

She'd wanted to get up before the sunrise so she'd be ready to harvest at the first rays of light.

It was still dark outside. She peeked into Elizabeth's room. The old woman was still snoring, and Heather didn't have the heart to wake her up.

She grabbed her coffee and notebook and padded to the

front porch. The screen door screeched, and she cringed at the noise.

She tiptoed over to the wicker rocker and sat.

The cool morning breeze made her shiver, but she was glad of it. Being out in the country made her feel alive, as if she were living for the first time in her life.

She didn't miss the smells of the city or the hardness of the buildings. Out here, it was different.

Everything was bursting with color and green grass. And the air smelled different, somehow sweeter.

She'd taken to leaving her window open as she slept. There was a time when she would never do that, for she knew the danger that could come through a window, whether it be a weapon or stranger intent on evil.

She didn't feel that here. Here she felt safe.

Here she felt at home.

Last night she'd even unpacked her few shirts and put them in an empty drawer. She still hadn't been able to unpack her backpack, but at least it was a start.

Endlessly moving around and not getting comfortable in one place had always made her feel like she was waiting for the other shoe to drop.

Harland Creek felt different. Something about the countryside pulled at her as if asking her to stay.

She shook her head. She couldn't bank on that, not just yet. She had to figure out how to line up another job once Elizabeth was better. Maybe she could find another elderly woman who needed help.

Her thoughts drifted back to Mrs. Ruth, and Atlanta, and promises that had been broken.

She did not miss her last job. Working in a dry cleaner had been hard and hot work, especially in the summer months of Georgia. It was little pay, but they didn't need you to have a college education and hard work was rewarded.

The owner, Mr. Griffin, had given her a small room in the back with a small cot. He'd seen the late hours she worked and told her she could spend the nights there if she ever worked late. He didn't like her walking to the bus stop after eleven. The city was too dangerous.

She'd been living with two other roommates who had aged out of the foster system in a low rent but cramped apartment. She managed to make the rent most months but barely had enough money left over for food. When Mr. Griffin had given her the back room to sleep in, she made it permanent and moved out of the apartment. He hadn't said much about her practically living there. Why would he? She got up early and worked late into the night. She was his most productive employee. She hadn't made any friends with her work ethic, but she didn't care. She had to survive, and saving money until she could figure out her future was of utmost importance.

Her life changed the day Ruth came into the dry cleaner with a lacy tablecloth.

She would always bring in tablecloths to get cleaned.

She was a twig of a woman, with white hair and an infectious smile. She always made Heather's day brighter when she came in.

One day, she called instead of coming in, asking if her dry cleaning could be delivered. Mr. Griffin, the kindhearted man he was, told Heather to deliver it in one of the business cars.

When Heather pulled up to her house, she was amazed at the little yellow house with a picket fence.

When she rang the doorbell, Ruth answered the door with a walker.

She'd gotten dizzy and fallen. Her doctor recommended she get someone to stay with her, but instead she'd gotten a walker. She invited Heather in. She hesitated at first, but

Ruth was insistent and called Mr. Griffin so she wouldn't get in trouble.

They'd had tea and cookies on pretty china and delicate cups.

It was her first tea party.

She smiled to herself as she thought about the memory.

"Something amusing?"

The deep tone of Grayson's voice startled her. She pressed her hand to her chest and jumped up out of the chair. "I didn't hear you drive up."

"That's because I didn't. I rode my horse over." He pointed to a chestnut-colored horse tied up by the big tree in the backyard.

Her gaze darted from him to his horse. She leveled a glare at him. "What are you doing here?"

"I'm helping Elizabeth with the harvest today." His boots made heavy thuds on each step.

"She said she had some volunteers coming. I thought she was talking about the high school students."

He grinned and for a moment she forgot how much she disliked him. "They are. We got about ten coming. Excited about getting out of school for the day. I know she's moving a little slow these days so I thought I would come lend a hand. I usually do it when I'm harvesting for Olivia's shop." He shrugged.

"How very neighborly."

"You know what would be neighborly? Some of that coffee. Ms. Elizabeth says you make great coffee."

"Really?" Her eyes widened.

"Yeah. I can get it myself." He reached for the screen door handle.

"Wait." She jumped up. "I'll do it. I don't want you waking her up with your loud boots."

She padded inside and headed for the kitchen. She

quickly poured him a cup of coffee. She grabbed a few packets of sugar and the ceramic cow pitcher of cream.

She slipped outside.

He had sat in the wicker chair beside hers. She held out the coffee.

"Thanks. I appreciate it."

"I didn't know if you wanted anything in your coffee." She set the sugar and cream on the little table beside his chair.

"Thank you."

She watched him dump two packets of sugar and pour some cream into his coffee.

"By the look on your face, you don't know many men that take their coffee like that."

"I don't know many men at all, so I have no opinion on the subject." She curled her feet underneath her and took a sip of her coffee.

"How are you up so early?"

"How are you?" she countered.

"I usually get up this early. I feed my cows and check on my other animals."

She nodded. "I set the alarm early so I could get organized as to what needs to be done to harvest." She picked up her list.

"You always make lists?"

"I like to know what needs to get done. I don't want to forget anything. There are steps and I need to know what comes next. I've never harvested before."

"I wouldn't stress about it. Just make sure you wear your boots."

"Boots?" She straightened and looked at him.

"Yeah. It's going to be muddy, and you need to wear rubber boots."

She racked her mind, trying to think if she'd seen any rubber boots in the closet.

"I think Elizabeth has an extra pair in the barn. I'm sure you can use those."

She nodded, feeling her anxiety resolve.

"Just be sure to dump them out before you put your foot in them. Never know what kind of critter you'll find."

"Critter? Like what?"

"Like a spider or frog or a bat."

"A bat? They live out here?" She pulled her T-shirt up over neck and looked skyward.

He let out a laugh.

She cut her eyes at him.

"Sorry. I forget you're a city girl. Besides, a bat is going to be more scared of you than you are of it."

"I doubt that. I'm not the one trying to bite him."

He laughed.

She relaxed a little and set the wicker rocker in motion. "Have you always done this?"

"Helped with the harvest? Yes. Ever since Elizabeth started planting flowers." A slight smile crossed his lips. "She didn't ask for help. She's too proud for that. But I got around that by explaining that Olivia needed a big shipment and wanted me there to make sure I got her the best of the best of the flowers. After that, she didn't complain about the help."

"Olivia's really good at her job. How did she know that's what she always wanted to do?" Heather sipped on her coffee.

"She didn't. In fact, she went to school for nursing. Worked at the hospital about a year. Then quit. She wanted to do something different. Said that she couldn't handle nursing." Grayson shrugged.

"Really? I would have thought she would make a great nurse. She's very intuitive when it comes to people. The way she knew what kind of arrangements to make with just a few basic instructions was genius." She frowned. Why couldn't she have a talent that would turn into a job and a future?

"I was just as surprised as you when she said she was giving up nursing. She seemed to be depressed about it for a while." Grayson frowned and looked out into the yard. "I wonder if it wasn't something else…"

"Something else what?" She looked over at him.

"Never mind." He shook his head. "What matters is she is good at what she does."

"I can't argue with you on that."

"So what are your plans after Ms. Elizabeth is all better? You moving on to bigger things?"

She looked down into her coffee. "I don't know. I haven't given it much thought."

"I'm sure you'll want to get back to your family and friends."

She glanced away. "I don't have family."

"Well, I'm sure your friends miss you."

She stood and gathered her notebook and coffee cup. "I need to get changed and fix breakfast for Ms. Elizabeth before we get started."

When he didn't move, she grimaced. "You are welcome to have breakfast with us. It's just basic eggs and toast. Nothing fancy."

"I ate before I came over here."

"You did? That's pretty early for breakfast."

"I'm used to it. I get up with chickens."

"You have chickens?"

He laughed.

She blinked.

He sobered. "Actually, yes, I have some chickens and cows and just got a couple of baby goats."

"Baby goats!" She spun around.

"Do you have much experience with baby goats?" He frowned slightly.

"No. But I've seen so many pictures of baby goats online. They look so sweet."

"They are when they're not trying to jump on my truck."

"Maybe you should build them something to climb on." She smiled. "Like a playground."

"Would a couple of old tractor tires do?"

"It would be better than them jumping on your truck." She grinned.

"I agree. You'll have to come see them. Olivia brought them some daisies. Which they promptly ate, of course." He rolled his eyes.

"Maybe I'll do that." She glanced into the house. "I better get breakfast started. I see Ms. Elizabeth's light on in her room."

"I'll gather the buckets and get things ready. No rush on you two getting out here. Enjoy your breakfast. Might be the only meal for the day." He jogged down the front porch steps and headed toward the old barn.

CHAPTER 16

*H*eather swiped a dirty hand across her forehead and forced an escaped tendril behind her ear. She and ten other workers, including Grayson, had been harvesting the tulips for over five hours now. She'd been surprised to see some familiar faces. Olivia had come around eight to help. She had left Amy in charge of the flower shop. She said she wanted to make sure she got the best tulips before her competition did. A friend of Olivia's also showed up. Her name was Tabitha and she was stunning. Agnes had gotten there early and had said her niece from New York had arrived unexpectedly late last night. She hoped Gabriela would be there but was sleeping when she left the house. George was sixteen and it was his first time to harvest. His dad was deployed overseas, and he was helping his mom with the bills so he needed the work. Michael, another high schooler, along with his buddy Walker arrived around seven, both more eager for a paycheck than doing a good job. After some stern words from Grayson, the two boys got their act together and were doing their fair share.

The cooler truck had arrived right after they'd finished breakfast.

She helped Grayson fill the buckets in the barn halfway with water. She got the harvesting system down after Elizabeth had gathered everyone and reviewed how the process worked.

They would cut the tulips at a forty-five-degree angle and strip any leaves that might fall below the water line. Once the bucket was filled with tulips, the runner, Georgie, would take the tulips to the cooler truck and bring back an empty bucket with water. By eleven o'clock that morning, the truck was overflowing with tulips of every color.

"Olivia, did you get the tulips you needed for the shop?" Elizabeth eased onto the tailgate of Grayson's truck.

"For this week. I also have orders from all the churches in Harland Creek to provide flowers for Easter. The country club also needs tulips for their spring luncheon." Olivia pointed to the numerous white buckets of tulips under the shade of the large oak tree. "This will get me through this week. I'll come back this evening and help. Right now, I've got to get back and make sure Amy got those deliveries out instead of flirting with the delivery guy."

"If you can't come back this evening, I understand." Elizabeth gave her a tired smile and rubbed her hip.

"Are you kidding? You couldn't keep me away." Olivia smiled and looked over at Heather. "You're a pretty good worker. I think you even made up for Tabitha's lack of work."

"Hey, I can't help it if I get distracted easily." Tabitha ran her hand through her long red hair. "Plus, I'm starving. I can't concentrate when I'm hungry."

Agnes snorted.

"Well, would you look at that." Tabitha shaded her hands as a young woman walked out between the line of parked cars.

"Is that?" Olivia cocked her head.

"It's Gabriela." Agnes scowled.

Heather watched, fascinated with how beautiful the woman was. She had long dark hair, almost black, and wore no makeup. She didn't need it. She had on jeans and a white T-shirt that was too small and showed her slender midriff. She was tall and walked like she owned the world.

"Well, missy. I see you finally rolled out of bed," Agnes snarled.

"I'm not much of an early bird." Gabriela sighed.

"Hi, Gabriela. Welcome back to Harland Creek." Olivia smiled.

"Thanks, Olivia. Although I'm not sure how long I'll be staying." Gabriela's gaze zeroed in on Heather. Heather looked away.

"You look like a million bucks, honey." Elizabeth nodded. "Come give me a hug."

Gabriela grinned and wrapped her arms around her. "You're very kind. How are you doing? Aunt Agnes said you had hip surgery. Feel up to going out dancing?"

Elizabeth barked out a laugh. "Not even when I was young. Gabriela, this is Heather Smith. She's staying with me while I recover fully from hip surgery." Elizabeth introduced her.

"Hi," Heather said quietly. Something about Gabriela's gaze made her think the woman could uncover every secret.

"Nice to meet you." Gabriela held out her hand.

Heather was surprised at her grip. She may look like a lithe model, but she was obviously strong.

Heather looked at Elizabeth who was favoring her hip. "I think you need to go sit down. I'll make you something to eat."

Elizabeth tried to wave her off, but Agnes came to Heather's defense.

"She's right, Elizabeth. You've been out there right along with us. You don't want to hurt yourself and delay your recovery time. Come on, I'll help you inside. I'll make you a cup of tea before I leave."

"Fine, fine." Elizabeth shook her head. She looked at everyone. "Thank you for all the help today. We'll start harvesting again in the evening. I'll be passing out paychecks after that."

She let Agnes lead her back to the house.

"You're not from here, are you?" Gabriela cocked her head.

Heather turned around and realized everyone was heading for their cars. Except Gabriela.

"No. I'm not." She started for the house.

"Where are you from?"

Heather forced a smile. "Georgia."

"That's a long way from home. How'd you manage to get way down here in Mississippi?"

"I found an ad in the paper about a caregiver. I wanted a change. I thought the idea of living in the country sounded ideal."

"Not much of a city girl, are you?" Gabriela snorted. "I don't blame you. The city will eat someone like you up and spit you out."

Heather lifted her chin. "Is that why you're not in New York anymore?"

Gabriela's eyebrows raised.

Heather regretted her choice of words. She didn't need to make any enemies here. She just needed a chance for everyone to get to know her.

"Pretty much. Or maybe I spit the city out." She shrugged. "Aunt Agnes said you didn't have any proper clothes for church."

Heather felt her face heat with embarrassment. "I've not gotten around to shopping…"

"She said she let you take one of the blouses I sent back for the auction."

"Yes. I have it in my room. I have been meaning to give it back…"

"Don't bother. When you have time, come over and go through my clothes. I've got too many clothes, and I'm trying to thin it out before I leave."

"You aren't staying?" Heather frowned.

"This isn't my town anymore. But you wouldn't understand that." Gabriela looked away.

"I might understand better than you think," she blurted out.

Gabriela studied her for a second. "I guess you've heard about me."

"I heard you got a modeling contract and left for New York after graduating high school. Sounds like you are living the dream."

Gabriela's eyes grew sad. She wrapped her arms around her thin chest.

"You're staying with Ms. Agnes? What about your parents?"

"My parents retired early and moved to Boca Raton. My mom always liked our vacations in Florida so after retirement, that's where they landed."

"You don't look old enough to have parents old enough to retire."

"I was actually a surprise baby. My mom had me later in life." She gave a ghost of a grin. Heather could see why the modeling agency hired her. She was beautiful when she was sad, but stunning when she smiled. "I'm an only child to older parents. My father and Agnes are brother and sister."

"I see." Heather nodded.

"What about you? Where are your parents? In Georgia?"

She shook her head. "No. They are gone."

"I'm sorry. I didn't mean to pry."

"It's okay. I'm hoping to find some work here in Harland Creek after Ms. Elizabeth is well. I'm not exactly sure where to start." She looked at the ground. "I didn't go to college after high school. Just went straight to work to make ends meet."

Oddly enough, she found herself opening up to the beautiful stranger.

"Like me. I personally think college is overrated, but what do I know." She tossed her hair across her shoulder.

Heather glanced over at the three high school students mulling around their trucks, trying their best not to be caught staring at Gabriela.

"I think your fan club is waiting on you." Heather nodded toward the boys.

Gabriela glanced over at the boys. All three perked up and smiled big. "Ugh. I'd rather go to one of Aunt Agnes' quilting bees than entertain men."

"Well, they're not exactly men. But why don't you come inside and have some tea while I fix lunch?"

"I'll take you up on it."

CHAPTER 17

The evening harvest didn't go as smoothly as the morning.

Elizabeth had been hurting and Heather insisted she take a pain pill and stay inside and rest. She'd been hard to convince, but when Grayson showed up, he'd agreed with Heather's assessment. The cooler truck had come back without any extra buckets. That sent everyone scrambling. Olivia volunteered the empty buckets from her shop and Grayson gathered every empty bucket he had on the farm. Word got out, thanks to Agnes, and Mac from the grocery store arrived with a truckload of plastic buckets. They worked well after dark, gathering as many tulips as possible. When the truck pulled out, arrangements had been made for them to come back in two days to pick up another shipment.

Elizabeth handed out checks to the three high school boys. She tried paying the others, but they all refused to take any payment from her.

Heather turned off the garden hose and picked up an old towel to dry off all the hand shears that had been used.

"Make sure you hang them up in the barn so they'll be dry for the next use. Oil them after the tulip harvest is done."

"Thanks for the tip." Heather bent to gather all the tools. "Elizabeth cooked dinner. You are welcome to stay."

He gave her a surprised look. "Are you sure it wouldn't be an inconvenience?"

"I have the feeling you know Elizabeth wouldn't mind. You've probably eaten at her table many times. So I'm guessing that question is aimed at me personally." She looked at him under her lashes.

He gave her a slow grin. She shifted her weight and looked away.

"Heather, I have a feeling you think I'm your enemy."

"Maybe it's the other way around. Maybe you think I'm the enemy." She lifted her chin.

"Why would you say that?" He studied her.

"You watch over Elizabeth like a hawk when I'm around her. Like you think I'm going to hurt her." She turned and gave him her full attention.

"I've learned the hard way that there are some people in this world that will hurt you. With her kids all living away, I feel like I need to watch out for her."

"Your mother would be so proud." She didn't keep the sarcasm out of her voice.

"I wouldn't know. My mother died of cancer seven years ago."

Guilt hit her in the chest like a baseball bat. "I'm sorry. I didn't know."

"How could you? You don't know me." He shrugged and gathered the hand shears. He started for the barn.

She waited a beat, unsure what to do. She hated that her words had been so callous.

She turned off the water hose and made her way to the barn.

She stepped through the door of the red barn. The scent of earth and fertilizer almost stung her nose in an odd way.

Grayson was busy hanging each shear up on individual hooks.

She swallowed her pride and walked over to him. She picked up a pair of shears and hung it up on the hooks.

"I didn't know my mother. Or my father for that matter." The words burned as they came out of her mouth. Not from fear of what he would think, but from allowing herself to be vulnerable for once in her life. It felt like jumping in the deep end of the ocean and not knowing if she remembered how to swim.

He turned and looked at her. "I'm sorry. That must have been hard."

"It was." She nodded and looked away.

"Are you an only child?"

"I... I don't know." She rubbed her dirty hands on her jeans. If she was going to make a home here, she was going to have to start making connections with people.

He blinked but didn't push her to talk.

"Grayson, Heather!" Agnes stepped into the barn. "There you two are. Dinner is ready. I tried to help Elizabeth cook, but darn if that woman ain't hardheaded." She scowled. "She barely allowed me to make the sweet tea and cornbread. The rest she did herself." She shook her head.

"I'm sorry. I should have done that." Heather hung up the last shear.

"Don't apologize. You helped more by helping with the harvest. I'm pretty sure you outworked everyone"—she pointedly looked at Grayson—"with the exception of Grayson."

"She certainly held her own. And for someone who had never harvested flowers before," Grayson agreed.

"Then come inside and eat. I'm headed home to get in the hot tub."

"You and Gabriela are not eating with us?" Heather asked.

"No, honey. I got into an argument with Gabriela and she headed home."

"Did she walk over here?"

"No, she rode her bike."

"It's ten miles from here." Grayson's eyes grew wide.

"I know. I made her pretty mad." Agnes shook her head. "I better get going and pick her up. Good night, you two." Agnes waved over her shoulder as she walked out of the barn.

"I take it they're not close."

Grayson snorted. "It's complicated."

She cocked her head. "So if they don't get along, why did Gabriela come home?"

"I don't know if she considers Harland Creek home." Grayson walked with her toward the house.

"That's hard to believe," she muttered.

"Some people are always looking for something better. Not a lot of people like small towns. Some think they are meant for better things." Grayson's voice hardened.

"I didn't get the idea from Gabriela that she thought she was better than Harland Creek."

"I wasn't talking about Gabriela." He stopped at the bottom of the stairs of the front porch.

"There you two are. Come on in before it gets cold." Elizabeth opened the screen door and held it open for them.

They hurried up the steps of the front porch.

"I'm sorry I didn't help cook dinner."

"Don't be sorry. I've never seen such a hard worker in all my days. You did good today." Elizabeth beamed.

Heather's chest bloomed with pride. "Thank you. That means a lot."

That night Heather lay in bed, exhausted. As she drifted off to sleep, she wondered at Grayson's words. He'd said some people were looking for better things. Who had he been talking about?

CHAPTER 18

"There has to be an easier way to harvest than by hand." Heather sighed as she straightened. She arched and stretched out her back.

While the first day of harvest had gone well, the second was not meeting the same expectation.

They were shorthanded when Michael and Walker didn't show up. Agnes was late. She apparently had some kind of bee emergency. Heather didn't have time to find out what that was about. To top it off, the cooler truck had been late arriving.

"They make a harvesting tractor but it's very expensive. They use it in Holland to harvest the tulips over there." Olivia swiped her hand over her forehead, leaving a dirty line across her head. Heather grinned and wiped the dirt off her face.

"Thanks. I'm always making a mess of myself." Olivia laughed.

"I can't imagine you ever being a mess. That title belongs to me." Heather arched her brow.

"What title is that?" Tabitha walked over. Her red hair was

in a tumble around her face. Despite that, she looked gorgeous.

"The title of who my brother is crushing on." Olivia snorted.

Heather went red. "That's not true." She looked at Tabitha.

Tabitha froze and then burst out laughing. "You're right, Olivia. That's why he didn't flirt with me yesterday. He is totally crushing on you, Heather. Olivia said he brought you to town the first day you arrived. He's been spending a lot of time over here."

"That's not true." She shook her head vigorously. "He's just being neighborly."

"What's not true?" Elizabeth pulled up on the golf cart that Agnes had brought over.

"We think Grayson is crushing on Heather." Tabitha beamed.

"Well, of course he is. They're both single and Heather's very pretty. It's about time he got over that Sarah girl." Elizabeth drove off.

"Who's Sarah?" Heather bent and started harvesting again.

"Ah, so he hasn't told you about that?" Olivia asked as she cut tulips.

"It's his ex-fiancée," Tabitha offered. Olivia cut her eyes at her. "What? It's not like she wasn't going to find out eventually."

"I didn't know he was engaged." Heather tried concentrating on her work.

"Was is the key word," Olivia said. "She wanted greener pastures and wanted to move to Memphis. Grayson wanted to stay here. So she broke up with him a week before the wedding."

"They didn't talk about where they were going to live when they got engaged?" Heather scowled.

"It was understood that they'd stay here. She knew Grayson would never leave his farm. She even got a job here. Until she went to Amber's destination wedding in Aruba." Olivia's voice hardened.

"I would think going to a wedding would make her even more excited to be getting married." Heather stood and looked at Olivia.

"Unless her friend Amber introduced her to one of the groomsmen who happens to be incredibly wealthy and they hit it off and spent every moment in paradise together." Tabitha sneered.

"You're kidding?" Heather shook her head. "Sounds like she's easily swayed by something so inconsequential as money."

"What are you girls doing? Hope it's not gossiping." Agnes parked the utility terrain vehicle that Grayson had driven over.

"We are." Tabitha brightened, not at all embarrassed at the woman's censure. "We're talking about Sarah."

"Oh. Her." Agnes narrowed her eyes. "Well, we only have a few more hours of daylight. The next cooler truck won't be here for two days, so we need to get as many tulips on this one as we can."

"In other words, you can gossip when the work is done." Tabitha nodded. "Got it."

Elizabeth and Agnes shook their heads and drove off to check on the others.

"Sorry, didn't mean to get everyone in trouble." Heather grimaced.

"You didn't. It's not like everyone doesn't know about it. This is a small town." Olivia shrugged. "And in small towns, all the secrets eventually come out."

The rest of the week, Heather quickly fell into a routine. On the days Elizabeth had her physical therapy, she would head out into the fields to check on the flowers. She kept meticulous records of which flowers to fertilize and when. When she thought some areas needed more water than others, she confided to Elizabeth. Usually, she would agree with Heather's findings. On rainy days she used her time deep cleaning the house and cooking. She worked so hard even Elizabeth said she made her tired just watching her.

She decluttered and organized the kitchen, helped Elizabeth display some of her finished quilts in the living room, and helped her with her exercises on the days the physical therapist didn't come. She was quickly getting comfortable in her new life. She just hoped it would last.

CHAPTER 19

*G*rayson poured himself a hot cup of coffee. He'd spent his time all week running between his farm and Elizabeth's. He would show up early to help with the flower harvest. And then go back to his farm to take care of his cows. He had a couple of cows who were due any day and he needed to keep a constant check on them to make sure there were no problems with the delivery of the calves. So far neither were ready to drop.

Thankfully it was raining today so they couldn't harvest any flowers. The break would give him some much-needed time to devote to the farm.

His cell phone buzzed with a text.

He picked it up.

"Are you with Heather?" ~Olivia

"No. Why would I be?" He sent back. It ruffled his feathers. Olivia had been hinting every day since Heather arrived that he had a thing for her. He loved his sister, but she needed to keep her nose out of his business.

Heather wasn't from here. She would see no future in a small town like Harland Creek.

"Just wanted to see if she's going with Elizabeth to the quilting bee tonight." ~Olivia.

"Like I said. I'm not with her."

He sent the text and scowled.

His phone rang. He picked it up without looking at the caller.

"Like I said, I'm not with her."

"With who? Sounds like I'm missing a lot of information here." Sam chuckled.

"Sorry. I thought you were Olivia." He ran his hand through his hair.

"So I gathered. Who does your sister think you are with?" Sam asked. "Or can I guess?"

"Heather."

"Ah, the beautiful new girl in town. I haven't seen much of her."

"She's been busy with Elizabeth. From helping with the harvest to taking care of Elizabeth. I'm guessing she's not been to town since the first day she arrived."

"Think she'll go to the quilting bee tonight?"

"Heaven help her if she does." Grayson finished his coffee and poured himself another cup.

Sam chuckled. "I'm hoping to finish the fellowship hall before they arrive."

"Yeah, you don't want to get caught up in all of that gossip," Grayson warned.

Sam laughed. "For once I can safely say I'm not going to be part of the topic tonight. If I were a betting man, I'm guessing they'll be talking about you and Heather. I just called to tell you I saw a car for sale in the paper. Tell Justin to check it out. It might be what he needs for college."

"I'll do that. Thanks."

"Later." Sam ended the call.

Grayson shoved his cell phone in his jeans pocket. Surely

they would not be discussing him and Heather. He shook his head. He knew this town and its people like the back of his hand.

The Harland Creek Quilters might be God-fearing women, but they had a penchant to make a mountain out of a molehill.

He just hoped they would keep their focus off Heather and his relationship.

CHAPTER 20

"*W*atch your step there." Heather supported Elizabeth as she stepped into the fellowship hall at the back of the church.

The scent of something wonderful filled the room. Ten older women were busy putting a colorful quilt in what looked like a large frame.

"I would have thought I would be getting less sore by now. But after this week, I'm feeling every step." Elizabeth grimaced.

"Maybe I should take you home." Heather had tried to talk Elizabeth out of going to her quilting session, but it was the first time since her surgery that she was attending and she didn't want to miss it. So Heather had relented.

"No, no. I'll be fine. Besides, the longer I'm babied, the longer I'll be dependent on you."

"And that's a bad thing because?" Heather arched her brow.

Elizabeth smiled. "You probably aren't used to being around an old grump like me."

"I'll take old grump in the country over fake happy in the city any day."

Elizabeth barked out a laugh.

"What's so funny? Y'all aren't gossiping about me, are you?" Agnes toddled over. She was wearing her weird bee hat and overalls. Buzzing around the brim of the hat was a honeybee.

"Not yet." Elizabeth gave her friend a playful look. "Heather, can you get that fabric out of the car?"

"Sure. Why don't you sit here?" She pulled up a white plastic chair and made sure Elizabeth was sitting before hurrying back to her car.

The cool spring air stung her lungs, but she liked it. She'd never smelled anything so sweet. It was like she'd stepped into another universe.

It was the only place she'd felt like she could stay forever.

Her gaze landed on her Georgia license plate. And her heart fell.

They were supposed to take Elizabeth's truck but getting in had proven more difficult this time. She knew Elizabeth was sore from the tulip harvest. So it was decided to take her car.

Her car. It tied her to her old life. Something she didn't want to even think about anymore.

It also tied her to her secrets about who she really was.

The people of Harland Creek had normal, stable lives. Unlike her. If they knew who she really was, she'd never fit in.

"Hey, Heather."

She looked up from gathering the material out of the trunk of her car. It was the guy from church. Grayson's friend. "Hello. It's…"

"Sam."

"Right. Sam. Sorry I didn't remember your name. I had so

many people coming up to me after church. It's a lot of names to remember." She gave him an apologetic smile.

"No problem. I don't offend easily." He grinned.

"Thanks." She shut the trunk. "Are you here to quilt too?" she joked.

"Not on your life. I'm just finishing up the construction on the fellowship hall. I had to pick up some tools so the ladies could get their quilt set up."

"You did the work in there? It looks great." She nodded.

"Thank you."

"As a contractor, do you find a lot of jobs here in Harland Creek?" She cocked her head.

"More than you know. I try to keep at least three jobs going at one time. Right now, I'm redoing a bathroom for a newlywed couple in town, building an outdoor kitchen for the pastor, and building a float for the upcoming parade."

"Parade? What's the celebration for?"

"Founders' Day celebration. Harland Creek has one every year."

"Are there enough people to participate?"

"There are. We have the marching bands from the surrounding towns march, as well as the local 4-H. We also have a horse riding association that rides their horses. We also have a horse-drawn covered wagon. We used to let the kids ride their four-wheelers, but the horses didn't like it too much so we put them in the end of the parade. And then there are the floats."

"How many floats do you have? And do you build them all?"

He laughed. "I do not build them all. Olivia is the only one who does a proper float. She does a theme every year and orders enough flowers from Elizabeth to incorporate it into the float. This year she is doing one that looks like her building, Roses and Lace. There are even window boxes with real flowers and a wheelbarrow with tulips in them."

"I bet it's pretty."

"It will be when I'm done. She usually gets a big uptick in sales after the Founders' Day Parade. We also have vendors set up along the town square where you can buy the best food you'll ever eat."

"Like something out of a movie. Sounds too good to be true."

"Well, I wouldn't say that. I mean, there is usually some drama."

"Drama? Like what?" Heather leaned in slightly.

"Well, Agnes got into an argument when Farmer Smith's prize pig got away from him and ate two large jars of her honey. She had a stand on Main Street and left it for just a minute to get a corn dog. When she came back, the pig was a sticky mess. You should have seen her give him what for." His grin widened.

"I bet it was quite a show." Heather knew how spirited the old woman was. She would let no one intimidate her.

"It was. The town was talking about it for weeks until something else caught their attention." He shrugged. "Well, good luck with the Quilting Bee ladies." He gave her a wave and slid into his truck.

She headed back inside where the women had gotten the quilt into the frame and were putting chairs around it.

"Heather, you know some of the ladies here." Elizabeth waved her over to where she was sitting at the quilt.

"Not me. She hasn't met me. We've not been introduced." An older woman with long salt-and-pepper hair eyed her carefully. "My name is Bertha Mills, and your name is?"

Heather knew the name sounded familiar but wasn't sure where she 'd heard it before.

"I'm Heather Smith."

"Oh yes. Heather. The nurse for Elizabeth." She eyed her up and down. "You're mighty young for nursing. Where did you get your license?"

"I'm not a nurse. I'm a caregiver. You don't need a license for that," she said quietly.

"Heather, come sit next to me." Agnes patted the empty chair between her and Elizabeth.

"I wasn't going to stay." She eased closer to Elizabeth.

"Come on. Just stay for a little bit." Agnes leaned in close to her and whispered, "Don't eat the tuna casserole. Bertha made it."

She blinked. "Wait, you mean the same Bertha who made the pound cake?"

"The one and the same," Agnes whispered.

"Heather, I'm Mildred." A gray-haired lady patted her on the shoulder. "Elizabeth tells me you are trying out our quilting bee to see how you like it. I'm so thrilled to see a young person with us today."

Heather cut her eyes at Elizabeth. The older woman was wearing a smirk.

"Yes, well, I have never quilted. Maybe I'll just watch." She nodded.

"Absolutely not. We are going to get you started. You'll be a quilting pro by the time you leave." Mildred lifted her chin confidently.

"I highly doubt that," she muttered.

After everyone took their seat, Mildred kept standing. "Good morning, ladies. As you see, we have Elizabeth back with us after her surgery. We certainly missed you." Everyone agreed.

"It's good to be back. Hopefully I'll be back to normal within a few weeks."

Something tugged in Heather's heart. A few weeks and she'd be out of options for a job.

"And we also have a guest with us as well. This is Heather Smith. She is staying with Elizabeth while she recovers."

Everyone smiled and offered their greetings.

"Hello, everyone." She ducked her head.

"Let's go around the room and introduce ourselves to Heather." Mildred looked at Heather. "And don't feel bad if you don't remember some of our names. We're old. We won't remember to be offended."

Everyone laughed.

"Since she already knows Agnes and Elizabeth, let's start with Bertha."

"I'm Bertha Mills. I was born and raised in Harland Creek. I am a retired city clerk. I use my retired time making baked goods for the elderly shut-ins."

"Those poor people," Agnes muttered.

"Hi, Bertha." Heather tried to hide her amusement.

"I'm Lorraine Chisolm. I am retired as well. I was a nurse for Dr. Vaughn for almost forty years. Now I spend my time gardening and quilting and volunteering at the nursing home."

"Hi, Lorraine." Heather immediately liked the white-haired woman. She had soft gray eyes, a genuine smile, and wore a pink jogging suit.

A twig of a woman wearing a blue twin set gave a slight wave. "Hi, Heather. My name is, well, it's odd. Let's just say people call me Weenie. Weenie Dunst. I am a retired librarian but work part-time at the English Rose bookstore on the square. Glad to have you here."

"Thank you, Weenie."

"Hi, there. My name is Donna Williams. I'm a retired schoolteacher. Now I tend to my vegetable and flower garden."

"Come on, Donna. Don't be so modest." Mildred grinned.

"Heather, Donna has won first prize on her vegetable and flowers every year at the county fair."

"Well, that's because Elizabeth refuses to enter." Mildred gave Elizabeth a nod. "I am grateful she doesn't enter; otherwise, no one would have a chance to win against her. Thank you, friend."

"You're welcome." Elizabeth chortled.

"And Donna also tutors high school seniors for their college exams."

"Right now, I have a break so I can quilt more." Donna nodded.

"We've met briefly on the square, dear. I'm Sylvia Jenkins." Sylvia waved. "I believe you were with Grayson."

A murmur rose up in the room. Her face heated.

"He was taking me to the grocery store since I didn't know my way around," she assured them.

"Interesting," Sylvia muttered. "As you know I am part owner of S&M beauty salon."

"Ugh. I can't believe you named your shop that." Bertha glared. "It's disgusting."

"Get over yourself, Bertha." The other woman who'd been on the square that day turned and gave Heather a smile. "Hi. I'm Maggie Rowe. The other owner of said disgusting salon."

Agnes snorted.

"Hi, Maggie." She bit her lip to keep from laughing.

Bertha was shooting daggers at everyone who was snickering.

"And I'm Mildred Agnew. I'm the owner of Mildred's Stitching Quilt Shop. I started the quilt bee a few years ago. It started out just once a month and then quickly turned into once a week. We make our blocks at home, and then I put them together and we hand quilt them here."

"How nice. What do you do with the quilts once you are finished? Do you sell them?"

"Oh no, dear. The ones we do here we give away. This one here is called Stars and Stripes. We are making it for Mr. Brooks. He's a war vet who turns ninety-five this year. It's his birthday present."

"Wow, that's amazing." She looked at the pattern of stars in red, white, and blue on a cream background fabric.

"Can we get started? I'm not here for some kumbaya session," Agnes groused.

Mildred shook her head. "Everyone have their needles ready?"

Everyone said they did.

"Here, Heather. I threaded your needle. I'm going to sit on the other side of you and show you how to hand stitch."

"I hope you are keeping your expectations low. And the Band-Aids handy." Heather shook her head.

"Be positive, dear. Everyone can sew." Mildred smiled brightly.

"I wouldn't be so sure," she muttered.

After numerous attempts at a proper stitch, multiple finger sticks, and too many drops of blood on the beloved quilt, Heather was encouraged to take a break and grab something to eat.

She quickly complied.

"I found some pads under the sink." Lorraine held out the feminine hygiene product.

She cringed and pressed the pad to her finger. "Thanks. Sorry about your quilt. I hope you can get the blood out." She bit her lip.

"Of course we can. Mildred had a special solution to get out any kind of stain," Lorraine reassured her.

"Good. I would have hated to ruined Mr. Brook's birthday present."

"I'll let you in on a little secret." Lorraine leaned in close. "The quilts are far from perfect. If you look at everyone's stitches, they are all different. Some are very tiny, some are too big, most are irregular. But that's what makes a quilt a quilt. All the imperfections. It's like life." She patted her on the shoulder and left her by the pound cake.

"Hungry? I made some pound cake." Bertha walked up and picked up a saucer. She reached for the knife.

"Oh, no, thank you. I'm gluten intolerant." She walked over to the hot tea and fixed two cups.

She walked back over to Elizabeth and handed her and Agnes a cup.

The women thanked her and took a break from quilting.

Heather fixed herself a cup and sat back down.

CHAPTER 21

"*T*hat certainly took a turn." Heather looked at Elizabeth wide-eyed.

"Certainly did." Elizabeth gave her a pointed look. "I knew that Bertha Mills was a troublemaker. I can't believe she called the pastor on us. We were not doing a thing." Elizabeth lifted her chin.

"Well, that's not exactly true." Heather eyed her. "I mean everyone was talking about the next quilt. Which was called Drunkard's Path?"

"So?"

"Which led to people talking about the pastor's sister and her getting a DUI," Heather said slowly.

"Well, it's not like the whole town doesn't know. I mean it was in the paper. If it was in the paper, I don't consider it gossip," Elizabeth stated.

"But apparently the pastor does. And he happened to walk in when Agnes was talking about it. Which led to him to suggest the quilting bee needs to be moved to another location."

"It's all Bertha's fault." Elizabeth crossed her arms. "Now the pastor is mad at all of us."

"I don't think he's mad. I think he's hurt." Heather sighed heavily. "It's a devastating feeling knowing people you love are gossiping about you."

Elizabeth moaned. "Ugh. You're mighty smart for a young thing." She shook her head. "I have to make it up to him. I'll make him a casserole."

"Why don't you just talk to him. Or write him a note. That's what I would do." Heather shrugged and opened the car door. She hurried over to Elizabeth's side. "And after you do that, I would be looking for a new place to quilt."

"I think Mildred will probably let us quilt in her shop. She's got a room in the back." Elizabeth grimaced as she eased out of the car with Heather's assistance.

"Let's get you inside and get you something for the pain."

"Not the strong medicine. I think just Tylenol. I don't want to get dependent on them."

"Sure. Sounds good. I'll fix you some tea and some of those cookies I made yesterday." Heather helped her up the front porch stairs. "Want to sit out here?"

"Yes. Might as well enjoy the good weather while we can." Elizabeth sat in the wicker rocker.

Heather went inside and put the tea kettle on. She pulled out two teacups and saucers. She pulled down the ziplock bag with the sugar cookies she'd made last night under Elizabeth's instruction. After Elizabeth had gone to bed, she'd put some extra cookies in a separate ziplock bag and placed it upstairs in her room beside the peanut butter and the granola bars she'd brought with her. Old habits lingered and she hadn't been able to throw them away.

She didn't know what tomorrow held.

There had been days in foster care that the only food

she'd gotten had been spoiled. Or days she hadn't had food at all.

She turned off the tea kettle and quickly fixed two cups of English breakfast tea. She placed two cookies on both saucers and took them outside.

"Here we go." She handed Elizabeth a cup of tea with two sugar cookies hanging off the saucer.

"Thank you, dear." Elizabeth set the saucer on the wicker table and took a sip of tea.

"You're welcome." She eased into the chair. Easy silence flowed between them.

"We have a few more days of tulip harvest, and then we have to think about the other flowers." Elizabeth stared off into her flower field.

"What's the next flower to be harvested?" Heather set the rocker into motion.

"The gladiolus. There's a lot of demand for them, especially during wedding season."

"How many colors do you have? I know Olivia said something about white gladiolus being in demand."

"I have white, peach, yellow, yellow with orange throat, and a very deep red." Elizabeth smiled as she talked about her flowers.

"You must feel like you live in heaven," Heather blurted out.

"Heaven?"

"Yeah. I mean you wake up surrounded by all those colors. Even in winter, it still must seem like a wonderland." Heather sipped her tea.

"You know what, Heather? I think you're the only person who probably thinks that. Besides me, of course." Elizabeth smiled with pride.

"Surely not. How could anyone not want to stay here forever?" She shrugged and nibbled on her cookie.

"I ask myself the same question. Especially after my kids moved away. You know, back in my day, families stayed together. But as the jobs moved from farming to the city with factories, people moved away. They had to go where the jobs were. Sometimes I wish we could go back in time and realize how lucky we were back then. Even if we were poor in material things."

Her words resonated with Heather.

"Do you have any other jobs lined up after you are done with me?"

She ducked her head. Sadness filled her chest. "No, I haven't thought that far ahead."

"You know, I was wondering. I know you probably had your heart set on being a caregiver, but you are also a great worker here on the farm. You are a hard worker. I was wondering if maybe once I'm better, you would be interested in staying on as a caretaker of my farm."

"Are you serious?" Her heart beat like a drum in her chest.

"Well, I know I didn't hire you to be a farmhand. But maybe you could think about it."

"I don't need to think about it. I'll take it." She felt like she was going to float right off the front porch.

"I guess we should talk about where you'll be staying." Elizabeth frowned, looking lost in thought.

"Would you rather I find a place to rent?" Her voice was small.

"No, dear. I was just thinking the room you are in is the smallest room in the house. You could move to the room next door. It has its own bathroom. Of course we'd have to move all my sewing stuff into the room you are in. I've kind of made a mess in there."

"Okay. Would you like me to start working on that?"

"Yes. And we can start decluttering that room after dinner. Goodness knows I have packed stuff away in that room for years. It would be good to go through and get it cleaned up."

"Sounds like a plan." Heather eased back in her chair and sipped her tea. For once things were looking up. And it looked like she had found the home she'd always searched for.

CHAPTER 22

"*I* thought you'd be over at Ms. Elizabeth's." Mitch stepped up to the tee box and lowered his driver.

Sam had called and invited him to play golf. Mitch and Sloan showed up as well since they had the day off.

"She said she didn't need my help. She said that she had tripled the amount of volunteers today." Grayson slipped on his golf glove.

Mitch hit the ball straight down the fairway. He picked up his tee and laughed.

"What?" Grayson swung.

"The volunteers tripled because the entire high school football team showed up. I don't blame them. Tabitha, Gabriela, and Heather. It's like a triple threat of gorgeous."

Grayson hooked the ball and turned to glare at Mitch.

"What? You asked." He shrugged.

"How do you know this?"

"Olivia told Sam. And Sam told me. She just sent a text to Sam to let you know those young guys are drooling all over Heather. One even asked her to the prom."

"I'm pretty sure she's too old to go to a prom."

"Of course she is. She's closer to your age." Sam stepped up to the tee box gave him serious side-eye. He hit the ball straight and it landed on the green.

Sloan teed off next. He didn't drive it as far but it was straight.

The only one of them not able to concentrate long enough to hit the ball was him.

He jammed his driver back into his golf bag and got into the golf cart. Sam slowly drove them over to his golf ball while Mitch and Sloan drove over in their cart.

He slid out of the golf cart and grabbed an iron. He narrowed his eyes at his ball buried in some tall grass between two trees. He gritted his teeth and lined up his shot. He swung.

"Also heard Elizabeth was cooking up a big meal tonight and invited everyone to stay and eat," Sam called out.

Grayson cringed as his shot sailed farther away than he intended.

He glared at Sam. "I'm sure Heather won't allow her to do all that work. She's very protective over her. Plus, she won't be inviting those boys to stay."

"I don't know. Elizabeth is very strong-willed. She'll insist on feeding everyone. You know how she is. Didn't you eat with Elizabeth and Heather a few days ago?" Sloan asked.

Grayson slammed his iron into the golf bag. "You know my golf game would be a lot better if you all didn't talk as much."

"Are you sure about that? You're a pretty crappy golfer as it is." Sam deadpanned.

Grayson glared.

"I don't think it's my chatting that has your game off. I think it's the fact that you're bothered by all those guys hanging over there with Heather," Mitch teased.

Grayson glared.

"Look, man. Everyone knows Sarah did a number on you. The way things ended between you two was difficult. But you can't keep living in your own protective shell and not ever let anyone get close to you. You're going to have to put yourself out there if you want to find love again."

He bristled under Sam's words. "You're one to talk. When are you going to get a girlfriend?"

Sam looked away.

Grayson sighed. "Sorry, man. I didn't mean to pry."

"I guess we all have our own issues when it comes to women." Mitch lifted his chin defiantly.

"That's a statement I can get behind." Grayson grinned. "Now let's start playing some golf."

CHAPTER 23

"So, what do you think? Will Gabriela punch him in the face or dump her water on him?" Tabitha nudged Heather. "I can't believe guys that young think they have a chance with her."

"I can. They are young and stupid and full of courage. It's something that will get them in trouble one day." She shook her head.

"Well, I'm complimented that they still think I'm hot. I mean I'm pushing thirty." Tabitha shrugged.

Heather turned and stared. "You're kidding, right? I thought you were my age."

"How old are you?"

"I'm twenty-three."

"You look older."

"Thanks a lot." Heather snorted.

"I didn't mean it like that. I mean you have wise eyes. And you don't act foolish like the rest of us. To be honest, you're more mature than me. I can see why Grayson is drawn to you."

"Grayson is not drawn to me," she insisted.

"Want to make a bet?" Tabitha lifted her chin.

"Sure." She crossed her arms over her chest.

"I bet he'll have a lot to say about Riley MacDougal headed this way. I bet he's going to ask you to the prom. All I got was an invite to go to a movie. Dinner not included." Tabitha scowled.

Heather laughed.

"Oh, look. Riley is wiping the sweat off his head and making his way over here." Tabitha pretended to be harvesting the final tulips in the field. They had been working all day without a break. Elizabeth had said today was the last chance to harvest.

"Oh no." Heather bent and got busy cutting tulips.

"Oh, hey, Heather." Riley paused in front of her with his hands on his hips. "I wanted to talk to you."

Her heart sank. "I'm kind of busy right now, Riley. Can it wait?"

"It's important. Besides, it won't take long." He gave her a grin.

She stifled a groan. "Okay." She set down the shears and walked away from Tabitha to the end of the row for some privacy. She turned and faced him.

"So, I know you're new in town and all. And we are having this party down by the creek this Friday night. I was wondering if you'd like to go. You know to unwind and get to know some people."

"Thanks, but no thanks." She gave him a strained smile.

"Come on. It will do you some good. Get you off this old farm for a change." Riley grinned.

"I don't want to get off this farm. I happen to like it here."

He sobered. "That's not what I meant."

"Riley, how old are you?"

"I'll be eighteen in a couple of weeks." He smiled.

"Yeah? Well, I'm older than you. Much older." She cocked her head.

"That's okay. I like older women. In fact, I used to date a girl from The Cat's Meow Club off I-55."

She grimaced. "I'm pretty sure that's illegal."

"I won't tell if you won't." He gave her a wink.

"Yet, the answer is still no." She turned and walked back to a grinning Tabitha.

"Don't say a word." She narrowed her eyes at her new friend.

"I can't commit to that. I'm horrible at not speaking my mind. If I was a spy, the enemy would get all the information out of me." Tabitha shrugged. "So what did he say?"

She sighed heavily. "He asked me out. When I told him I was much older than him, he then told me he dated older women. One in particular from The Cat's Meow Club."

Tabitha's eyes bulged.

"Judging from your look, that's not a restaurant."

"No. it's not. It's a den of ill repute, as Elizabeth would say." She cocked her head. "And he's lying, trying to impress you."

"How do you know?"

"Well, I have it on good authority that Riley and his friends got into some trouble. Seems like the cops were called when they tried to present a fake ID at that club. They begged Sloan not to tell their parents. In exchange, they have to do volunteer work." Tabitha waggled her eyebrows.

"Volunteer work?"

"Yeah. Right here," Tabitha said.

"Does Elizabeth know?" She glanced at the front porch where Elizabeth was taking a break from the harvest. She'd wanted to stay out in the field with the rest of them, but Heather insisted she go rest. Finally, she had relented.

"Of course not. Nobody does."

"How did you find out?"

"Remember Allison, the one you met in church?"

"The beautiful blonde?"

"Yes, she's Sloan's sister. We usually eat dinner together once or twice a week. Anyhoo, Sloan slipped up and said something and I managed to pull the entire story out of him."

"So what you're saying is you would make a better interrogator than a spy?" Heather grinned.

"Yeah. Actually, I would." Tabitha grew serious as if she were contemplating the idea.

Heather laughed.

"Hey, what's going on?" Grayson pulled up on his side-by-side vehicle. He was dressed in golf clothes.

"Last day of harvest. Elizabeth said you had a lot of work to get done on your farm. I didn't realize that meant golfing." Heather narrowed her eyes.

His face turned red. "I got my work done early and Sam came by with some of the guys to ask me to golf. Said I hadn't been in a while. And I called Elizabeth to make sure she didn't need me. She said she didn't."

"Did Sloan and Mitch go with you?" Tabitha asked.

"Yes."

"Did you win?" Tabitha asked.

"Win? That's not exactly how golf is played." Grayson arched his brow.

"Oh yeah? Well, I know for a fact that Gabriela is a better player than all you guys put together. I bet she would win."

Grayson narrowed his eyes at Tabitha. Heather bit her lip to stop from laughing.

"I've never seen Gabriela play golf in all the years she lived here," Grayson said.

"That's because she picked it up in New York." Tabitha rolled her eyes. "I'm going over to speak to those boys to tell them to quit staring at you and get to work." She pointed to Heather.

Heather shook her head.

"Are they bothering you?" Grayson's tone was rough.

"They are just being boys. And I wouldn't lump them all together. Riley was the only one who asked me out."

"Riley?" He jerked his head toward the boy in question.

"He seems to think we're the same age." She shook her head. "I told him I'm way older than him."

"He's too young to understand that you should never ask a woman her age." Grayson crossed his arms over his chest.

"You did." She gave him a look.

"See. He should learn from my mistakes."

She laughed.

"You want me to give Riley a talking to?"

She looked over her shoulder. "Nah. I think he's moved on to greener pastures." Riley was now putting the moves on Tabitha. He must have said something, because the next thing Heather knew, Tabitha was dumping her water bottle over his head.

The rest of his friends rolled with laughter.

"Yeah, well, I better remind him exactly why he's out here. Sloan's not going to take too kindly to his actions." Grayson gave her one last look and walked toward the group of boys.

The way he looked at her made her stomach warm and tingly.

She'd never felt like that with anyone and it scared her.

She knew if she was going to make Harland Creek her home, she was going to have to start letting herself be vulnerable with the people.

Even with Grayson McCade.

CHAPTER 24

*H*eather stepped out of the shower and quickly toweled off.

The last day of tulip harvest had her hurting in places she didn't know she had.

And it felt terrific.

They had harvested for weeks. Tomorrow they would start focusing on the other flowers.

She towel-dried her hair and put her jogging pants and T-shirt on.

Over dinner she and Elizabeth had talked about decluttering the larger bedroom upstairs for her. And tonight they would start that project.

Since Elizabeth still couldn't manage the stairs, Heather would pack up the items and bring them down one box at a time.

She stepped into the room and turned on the light. She glanced around, taking in the bright room. Heather understood why Elizabeth picked this room for her sewing. The windows were large and would let a lot of light in, and the pale-yellow wallpaper looked like someone had plastered the sun itself in the room. She pushed the sheer white curtains to the side and looked out into the star-filled sky. She liked that the room wasn't modern or up to date. To her it felt like home.

Her gaze landed on the sewing machine sitting on a small table. She certainly wasn't going to be using that and figured Elizabeth would like to have it downstairs in her room.

She unplugged the machine and wrapped the cord and foot pedal up.

The stairs creaked as she walked down. "I think we should set up your sewing machine in your bedroom. You've got a small space by the window that would work well."

"That's a great idea." Elizabeth stood from the recliner and hobbled over to her room. She flipped the switch. "I think that sewing table is too heavy for you to carry by yourself."

She set the sewing machine under the window. "Not if I fold it up. I'll be right back."

She hurried up the stairs. She took the folded fabric and put it in one of the empty boxes that Agnes had brought over earlier. Once the table was clean, she set it on its side and folded the legs under. Testing the weight, she decided she could safely take it down the stairs.

"Be careful." Elizabeth's face was pinched in worry.

"I'm stronger than I look," she joked.

"I don't doubt that." Elizabeth let out a sigh once she had set up the table in the bedroom.

Heather set the sewing machine on the table and plugged it in. She looked around her room. "I can set the box of fabric under the table until we can organize it."

"Honey, I've never organized fabric in my life. I usually dump it out and find what colors I want to quilt with and go from there."

She grinned. "I'll go ahead and bring down the clothes in

the closet. That way you can go over what you want to keep and what you want to donate."

She hurried up the stairs and back into the bedroom. She dragged a large box over to the closet and turned the light on. It was deep enough for her to step into and was overflowing with clothes. She began piling the clothes along with their hangers. Next came the shoes. She piled them on top. There were some decorative boxes at the top of the closet she pulled out.

She'd bring the broom upstairs and give it a good sweeping out once she took everything down to Elizabeth.

"Here we go. All the stuff in the closet." She set the box down in front of Elizabeth who had taken a seat in the wingback chair beside her bed. "Don't start deciding on what you want to keep until I bring an empty box in here."

She went out on the front porch and grabbed an empty box. She found a pen and wrote *Donate* in large letters on the side.

"Now. This is the donate box." She pulled out all the shoes and handed them to Elizabeth. One was a sparkly pair with a fat heel. The other were old sneakers and one pair of shiny leather dress shoes.

"Are these in style anymore?" Elizabeth held up the sparkly heels.

Heather bit her lip.

"I want honesty," Elizabeth deadpanned.

"No. None of them are. If you donate them, someone might buy them for a costume or something."

"Fine." She chucked them into the donate box. "Next."

Heather grinned and pulled out two items. One was a large-sized floral blouse and the other a floor-length dress in a drab brown color.

"Maggie wore that for her high school graduation. And she wore that shirt all the time in the summer." Elizabeth cocked her head. "Should I keep it just in case she wants it?"

"This is early eighties at best. I don't think that fashion is ever coming back." Heather cringed.

"You're right. Donate." Elizabeth sighed.

They went through the clothes fairly quickly. Heather discovered some jeans in her size that Elizabeth said she should keep. There was one white dress with tiny roses that she liked. It was a size too large, but Heather didn't care.

"I can take it in for you. If I had the looks you have, I'd be wearing dresses every day." Elizabeth smiled.

"I don't know about that." Heather handed her one of the two decorative boxes.

"Oh my. I'd forgotten about this."

"What is it?" Heather sat at her feet and watched as she pulled off the lid.

A big smile broke out across her face. "It's my old church hat."

"Hat? Like the kind Agnes wears?"

Elizabeth laughed. "No, honey. It's my old Easter hat."

"Is that really a thing? To wear a hat for Easter?"

Elizabeth gave her a wide-eyed look. "Of course it is. In the South at least. When my kids were young, they would all get a new outfit for Easter Sunday. And Maggie and I would wear our Easter hats. See?" She pulled out the once white lace hat with a wide brim. There was a bow that tied at the back.

"Put it on and let me see." Heather grabbed a hand mirror off the dresser and held it out as Elizabeth tried on the hat.

"Oh my. Look at that old face staring back at me. It looked better when it was white and I was young. I wonder if I can bleach it and make it white again."

"I think you should just let it go. Unless you want to turn it upside down and use it as a planter." Elizabeth scowled and handed it to her. "You might change your mind once you see how it looks. Try it on."

She put the old hat on and looked at herself in the mirror. "I don't think it's my style." She took it off and handed it to her.

Elizabeth sighed. "I guess some things are unredeemable. Stick it in the trash."

Heather's stomach ached at the woman's word. "I wouldn't say that." She shrugged. "I mean what if you donated it? Someone might still want it and find it a good home."

Elizabeth shook her head. "I don't know if I want my hat in someone else's home."

"I think it would look very pretty on a little girl having a tea party. Once her mother dyed the hat pink, of course." Heather nodded encouragingly.

Elizabeth frowned. "Maybe I'll save it for John's little girl."

"That's a great idea. I'll put it over here in the keep pile."

"That was unusually refreshing. I think we've done enough for tonight. My physical therapist really worked my leg today. I think I'll head to bed." Elizabeth stood and stretched.

"Did you take your medicine?" Heather moved the donate box into the living room.

"I did, mother hen," Elizabeth groused.

Heather grinned and walked back into the bedroom. "Good night."

"Good night." Elizabeth headed into her bathroom to prepare for bed.

Heather gathered up her new-to-her jeans and headed upstairs. She opened her closet and frowned at the food stockpiled in the bottom. She hated that she still felt the need to hoard food for an emergency. She had three packs of crackers, peanut butter, and a small bag of cucumbers she bought from a neighbor who had a roadside vegetable stand. She'd also kept some granola bars which she'd had since her trip from Georgia.

She bent to gather the items up and put them in the kitchen but stopped.

Not quite yet.

She'd do it later. When it felt right.

When she felt like she was truly home.

CHAPTER 25

*G*rayson muttered to himself, "I can't believe Justin didn't walk the fence line. I told him he needed to do this last week." Now two of his cows had found a weak area in the fence where a tree limb had fallen after the rainstorm. They knew where greener pastures were with loads of flowers.

Elizabeth Harland's land.

Thank goodness he'd checked on the cattle at sunrise. Hopefully he could catch up to the two mischievous cows before they could do any damage to her flowers.

He heard the banging before he saw the scene.

"Get out of here!" Heather was standing between the cows and the field of what was left of the tulips. He noticed the sharp green heads of the gladiolus bursting forth from the ground.

She was wearing jeans and a white T-shirt and those rubber boots of Elizabeth's. She was banging on a metal bowl with a wooden spoon and looking to defend the flowers with determination in her face.

He grinned.

"Are they yours?" Heather called out, looking none too happy.

"I'm afraid so."

"Please tell me they don't eat flowers." Heather blocked a cow as it tried to walk around her.

"I'm afraid they do." He rode over to her to help block the cows. "My farmhand didn't walk the fence like I told him. I guess I should have double-checked the fence to make sure there wasn't any weak areas."

"Is there anything I can do to help?" She looked up at him.

"I think I can manage them on my own." He cut the cows off, but they tried to go the other way.

Heather jumped in front of them and started waving her hands.

The cows glanced longingly at the colorful field and finally turned around toward home.

"Heather, do you mind going with Grayson? I'm sure he's going to need help to make sure they get home," Elizabeth called from the front porch.

"Are you sure you don't need me?" Heather called out.

"I'm sure. Take the day off. I plan on getting some sewing in today. I'm behind on a lot of projects. No need to hurry back." Elizabeth smiled and pointed to the front porch. "And wear your sneakers. It's not muddy." She gave them a wave and closed the screen door behind her.

"Can I grab my sneakers really quick?" She looked up at him.

"Sure."

She hurried to the house and quickly slipped into her sneakers and then ran back to him.

He slid off the horse and held the reins.

"You're not going to ride?"

"Nah."

They had to cut the cows off a couple of times, but once

they realized they had no chance to turn back to Elizabeth's field, they fell into a slow walk back to Grayson's farm.

"You're up early." Grayson looked over at her.

"I went to bed kind of early last night. Harvesting really is hard work. But it definitely helps with a good night's sleep."

"Yeah. I'm an early bird myself."

"Really?"

"Yeah. Besides having to feed the animals early, I love watching the sun come up."

"That's what I was doing when I spotted the cows. At first I thought it was a monster coming over the hill. Until one mooed."

He laughed out loud.

She slapped his arm playfully. "I'm serious."

"Good news for you. These monsters are vegetarians."

The sunrise hung low in the sky. "I never thought I would love this time of day. I think it's because I've never seen it this way. Not out here in the country." She smiled.

"That looks good on you."

"What?" She glanced down at her shirt.

"The smile. You look… peaceful."

She ducked her head. "Maybe I am. Finally."

"Did something change?" His gut twisted.

"It did." She grinned. "Elizabeth asked me to stay on. Wants me to help her full-time with the farm."

Warmth spread through his chest. "Really?"

"Yes."

"And you feel like this is the place for you?"

"I've search for a place like this all my life. Someplace that feels like home."

"You sure you won't get bored?" He nudged Ranger when he stopped to munch on some grass.

She stared at him long and hard. "You know, Grayson. Some people can't be pleased. They are always looking for the next best thing. That's something I don't understand. What I want in life is to have a home, work hard, and at the end of the day have no regrets."

"And what about having a family? Do you see that in your future?"

"One day, yes. When I find someone who wants the same things I do. Someone who wants a quiet life."

He had so much he wanted to say but the cows were at the creek.

"Is this the famous Harland Creek?"

"It is. You haven't seen it?"

"No, I haven't had time to explore the land. It's smaller than I expected." She glanced down at her shoes. "Maybe I should have worn my boots."

"Nope. Here, get on Ranger. Ride across so you won't get your feet wet."

"I've never been on a horse before."

"It's okay. Ranger is gentle." He held out his hand. She took it.

"Now put your foot in the stirrup. And grab the top of the saddle and pull yourself up."

He helped get her foot in position and gave her a boost into the saddle.

She looked down wide-eyed. "How do I make him go?"

"Give him a gentle kick in the sides. Don't worry. He knows what to do."

She gave him a worried look but followed his instructions.

Ranger slowly walked across the small stream and up the bank to the other side where the two cows were waiting.

"HOLD RANGER here and let me herd them through the break in the fence." He herded the cows through the open spot in the fence. Once on the other side, they spotted the other cows and made their way toward them to tell them of their great adventure.

"Aww, you're a sweetheart," Heather said softly.

"Thank you." He turned around. His smile faded when he saw she was talking to and rubbing the horse.

She burst out laughing when she saw his face. "Sorry. I'm sure you're a nice guy too."

"Not a sweetheart?" He arched his brow.

"We'll see," she teased.

"Since you're here, you might as well come see the new babies."

"Babies?"

"Yes, I have two new calves. They were born during the night."

"I'd love to." Her eyes widened with excitement.

He grinned. He led Ranger through the downed fence. "Let me mend this fence first. Can you stay here while I run back to the barn with Ranger to get the supplies to fix it? Just make sure no one else makes a break for it?"

"Sure." She slid off the horse and gave him one final pat.

He hoisted himself up on Ranger and pointed the horse in the direction of the barn. The horse settled into a gallop. A few minutes later he was in his barn gathering supplies to mend the fence.

He put everything in the back of his side-by-side vehicle and drove back to Heather.

"That didn't take long." She walked over and looked in the back of the side-by-side.

"I was trying to hurry in case there might be a stampede."

Her face paled. "Is that possible?"

"No. I'm kidding." He chuckled.

"Funny." She smirked. "So, do you want me to hold this side of the fence while you mend it?"

"That would be great." He pulled some barbed wire out of the back of the all terrain vehicle and placed it on the ground. "Here, put these gloves on so you don't get stuck." He tossed her some leather gloves.

"What about you?"

"I'm used to getting cut." He shrugged.

He worked quickly while she held the fence in place. Not once did she complain.

Unlike Sarah. If she were here, she'd be constantly asking how much longer it was going to take.

He stepped back from the fence and looked at his work. "I should have walked the fence line instead of asking Justin. It's my responsibility and my farm."

"Everyone needs help. Besides, he works for you." She gave him a kind look.

"I know. Don't get me wrong. He's been a real asset. The downside is he's going back to college in the fall. He's busy lining up student loans and trying to see what kind of classes he needs. His truck just quit so he's also trying to find a good, dependable car."

"How long have you worked the farm?"

"All my life. My mom inherited it from her parents. My dad and mom worked it together until my dad died of a heart attack. I was in high school and worked before and after school."

"Wow. That doesn't make for much of a social life."

"I had a girlfriend before my dad passed. We grew up together. Started dating in high school. Were even engaged for a while. Until..." He glanced away.

"It's okay. You don't have to talk about it," she reassured him.

"I'm pretty sure you already know." He turned back to her. "This is a small town after all."

'Yeah, well, I'd prefer to hear it from you. That is if you want to tell me."

He hadn't expected that.

He shoved his hand through his hair. "Well, she went to a wedding, one of those destination weddings, and ended up with another guy. She said she wanted more than what Harland Creek had to offer. She came home long enough to get her things and…"

"And what?"

"I had opened a savings account and had been putting money away to buy a new tractor. Since we were engaged, I put her name on it too. She ended up taking it all." He bit his lip.

"Gosh, I'm so sorry. I didn't know."

"No one knows. Not even Olivia."

"Why?"

"Because it was a lesson for me in trusting blindly. I was more hurt than angry. And embarrassed for putting myself in that situation." He looked away.

"Did she ever give you a reason to think she wasn't happy here?"

"Looking back, maybe she did. But I had been too young and stupid to think she'd ever leave. I mean, this is home, right?"

"I understand." Heather uncrossed her arms and looked around the green pasture spotted with cattle. "Out here, everything is so vibrant and alive and beautiful. What more could you ask for?"

"Exactly." He stared at her. The morning breeze had picked up her blond hair, lifting it against the backdrop of the clear blue sky.

"So, what else do you have to do today? You said Justin was supposed to walk the fence line?"

"Yeah. I guess I need to take care of that today."

"Need some help?"

Out of habit he almost said he didn't need help. He didn't mind helping others but often felt weird about accepting help himself. But he caught himself.

"Help would be nice."

She smiled and he noticed how her eyes sparkled when she was happy.

He cleared his throat. "So let's just start here. Have you ever driven one of these?" He nodded at the side-by-side vehicle.

"No."

"It's just like driving a car. I'll let you drive down this side of the fence while I walk it. Go ahead of me and if you see an area the cows can get through, tie an orange string around it. You'll see it in the bed of the side-by-side."

She eased into the driver's seat. He showed her the ignition and how to shift gears.

"This is like driving a car. A mini car." She grinned.

"Something like that. But not as much power."

She started down the line as he walked behind her. After she had gotten more comfortable with the side-by-side, she went on ahead of him.

As he walked the fence line, he stole glances at Heather. She drove slowly and stopped a couple of times to tie a string around weakened areas of the fence.

He was finishing mending the last spot when she pulled up beside him.

"Have far do you want to go? Looks like this goes on for a ways."

"We'll stop here for today. I know you're wanting to get back to Elizabeth." He put the roll of barbed wire into the back of the side-by-side.

"She said I had the day off. I moved her sewing machine

downstairs to her bedroom. I'm sure she's going to be catching up on her quilts."

"I heard from Sam you went to the quilting bee at church. Is that something you are interested in?"

She laughed. "I don't think you want me anywhere near a needle. And I'm fairly certain the ladies don't want me back. I bled on their quilt." She cringed.

He grinned. "I don't think they are going to be quilting at church anymore. Heard the pastor told them to find someplace else to go."

"News travels fast." She arched her brow.

"Small town," he countered.

"Yes, it is." Her voice was soft and quiet.

"Let's ride over there. I think I see the new calves." He jumped in the passenger side and let her drive as he pointed in the direction of the babies.

"Oh, gosh. How sweet. And they are so big already. Will they let me pet them?"

"No, they pretty much stay close to mama."

He saw the disappointment in her eyes.

"Come to the house with me. I want to show you something." He slipped into the driver's side.

"What is it?" She frowned.

"Something you'll like. Something you can pet."

CHAPTER 26

*H*eather's breath caught in her throat when Grayson drove to the top of the hill.

Below it stood his white farmhouse and red barn.

"It's beautiful. It looks like a painting," she whispered.

"You think so?"

"Yes. It's the ideal farmhouse."

"Thanks. My grandfather built it for my grandmother. The only thing she wanted was a porch. So he built her one that wrapped around the whole house."

"Is she still alive?"

"No. She passed when I was a boy. She made the best peach cobbler, and my grandfather used to take me fishing. I caught my first fish on that pond over there." He pointed to the pond off in the distance.

"That's great to have so many family memories. You are very lucky."

He looked at her. "There's always time to make new memories."

She nodded.

He slowed as he headed for the barn. His horse Ranger came out and looked at them.

"Hey, boy." The second he stopped, she jumped out. The horse came right over to her.

"Well, that's new."

"What?"

"Ranger. He never is that loving with anyone except me."

"Is that right?" She rubbed his long nose and looked at Grayson. "Maybe he smells the flowers on me."

"I don't think that's it." He stared at her.

She turned her attention back to Ranger. "What did you want to show me?"

"It's in here." He headed to the red barn and opened the door.

Before she could make it inside, six tiny goats burst out. They ran over to the bales of hay that were stacked and climbed up and jumped off.

"Baby goats. How precious."

"If you sit, they'll come over to you."

She smiled and sat down on the ground. "Hey, baby goats. Come over…" Before she could get the words out, they had spotted her. They ran over and immediately began bleating. They climbed in her lap and jumped. One even managed to climb on her back.

"Oh, sweet!" She laughed as another goat chewed on her hair.

"Yeah, you'll change your mind when they are eating your clothes," he groused.

"I don't think I'd mind. They're too cute!" She laughed and cuddled the goats. She didn't even mind them chewing on her hair. "If I had baby goats, I would put pajamas on them."

"They would probably try to eat them off. They eat every-thing." He pointed at the barn.

"Here comes mama. It's time for them to eat." A larger goat came out of the barn, bleating loudly. Obviously, mama was trying to gather her children for breakfast.

Grayson held out his hand and she took it. He pulled her up and she realized how close they were standing. Her heart thudded in her chest. Fear and excitement flooded her chest as he held her gaze.

He brushed her cheek gently with his hand. "I have a confession. I've been thinking about you an awful lot. And if I'm being honest with myself, I have wanted to kiss you for a very long time."

She swallowed and took a step back. "Grayson, there's something I have to tell you."

"Okay."

"It's kind of embarrassing." She knew without looking in a mirror that her face was red.

"I won't laugh." His voice was gentle.

She opened her eyes. "I… I grew up in the foster system. Some homes were worse than others. I tried to keep to myself, and I never had a date. Not even for prom. Even if someone had asked me, I wouldn't have been able to afford a dress."

"That must have been hard." His voice was calm and gentle, and she didn't hear any judgment in his words. Just understanding and kindness.

"It was. That's part of the reason I came here. I wanted to find a place to call home. Some place where I could make a life."

"Harland Creek is a good place for it." He smiled.

"I'm telling you that because I've never been on a date, which means I've never been kissed. And don't know how." She squeezed her eyes shut tight.

"I haven't kissed anyone in a long time. So maybe I forgot how." He shrugged.

She opened her eyes and stared at him for a second. Then she burst out laughing.

He grinned and took her hand. "How about we hold off on the kissing right now. When you're ready, you can let me know."

"Okay." She nodded.

"Would you like to see the house?" He cringed. "It's been a while since a woman has lived in it. So don't expect much."

She squeezed his hand, liking the feel of his calluses against her palm. "I'm sure it will be fine."

As they walked up to the porch, a yellow dog that had been sleeping lifted his head.

"That's Titan. I've had him close to ten years. He used to have more spunk, but he's starting to show his age."

The dog didn't bark but looked at her carefully as she knelt beside him. She looked up at Grayson. "Can I pet him?"

"Sure. He's useless as a guard dog."

She rubbed his head, and the dog rolled over and gave her his belly. "Aren't you a good boy."

When she stood, Titan stood too, ready to follow her into the house.

"Come on, boy. We'll get you a dog bone." He held the door open for her to enter first.

She stepped inside, shocked at the light interior. "This is not what I was expecting. It's beautiful."

He laughed. "After my mom inherited the house, she updated it. She had shiplap installed on the walls in the living room and kitchen." He pointed to the walls. "She replaced the countertops with butcher block to keep the character of the house." He ran his hand on the counter. "Other than paint and some minor replacements, she tried to keep the house as similar to the time period it was built."

"I was expecting antlers and a gun over the fireplace." She arched her brow.

"Look in the dining room."

She poked her head into the dining room. The walls were painted a soft gray and white bead-board. The table was large and made of a dark wood. From the scratches she could tell it had seen a lot during its time. Her gaze drifted upward to the chandelier. It was made of antlers.

"My dad insisted on that." He added, "Want to see the rest of the house?"

"Absolutely."

She followed him as he showed her the house. There were three bathrooms, one of them off the kitchen, the other two near the three bedrooms which were located upstairs. The back porch led to an outdoor living area with a firepit and a long table and chairs.

"Grayson, this is beautiful. Did you decorate it yourself?"

"No, Olivia helped update it. If I had my way, I would cover everything in leather and horns."

She laughed and pointed toward a smaller red building next to the red barn. "What's that? Looks like a child's dollhouse."

He gave her a weird look. "Really?"

"Yes, it's so cute."

"It's a chicken coop."

"No, it's…" She stopped talking when a couple of chickens walked down a plank onto the ground. "But it's so cute. It has a window box of flowers." She looked at him.

He rolled his eyes. "Olivia's doing. She thinks she's being funny."

"Remind me to compliment her on her decorating skills." She grinned.

"Want to have a seat? I hadn't finished my coffee this morning when I noticed the missing cows."

"I'd love a cup."

"Cream and sugar?"

"Yes, please." She eased into one of the chairs surrounding the firepit.

A few short minutes later he returned with two mugs of coffee.

"Thank you." She took the hot brew and settled back into the chair. "Do you sit out here a lot?"

"Every chance I get. Which lately isn't very often. Between running my farm and helping with the flower harvest, I've been going to bed early."

"Well, now that I know what I'm doing with the harvest, you won't have to help as much. You'll be able to focus on your farm. You might think about hiring a part-time worker after Justin leaves for college. Maybe some high school student."

"I don't know. Usually Elizabeth snaps them up. She'll still need help after she's healed." He took a sip of his coffee.

She bit her lip. "Maybe not, since I'm staying on."

A smile broke out across his face. "That's true. I hope you don't grow tired of living in the country."

She sighed, contentment rising in her chest. "This is the first place I've ever been that feels like home to me."

"That's the best news I've heard all day... all year."

She looked at him and her heart sped up, like it always did. Except she knew it wasn't from nerves.

She was falling for him.

"Heather." He stood and held out his hand.

She took it. "Yes?" The intensity in his eyes made her chest ache. She'd never felt anything like this in her life.

"I want to kiss you."

Seconds passed.

"What are you waiting for?" She frowned. Had he changed his mind?

His lips tugged into a lazy grin. "No. I just want to make sure it's okay with you. I want you to trust me."

"Okay." She placed her hands on his hard chest.

He cupped the back of her head and bent his head. His lips brushed across hers, gentle and unhurried.

When he finally pulled back, they were both breathless.

"I have to be honest. I haven't felt this strongly about anyone." He stared intently at her.

"Not even Sarah?"

"Not even Sarah."

He brushed a stray hair out of her eyes. "I'd like to take you to dinner Friday night. At Loftin's."

"Where is that?"

"On the square. It's nice. I've only been there twice with Olivia and Sam. I even wore a tie." He grinned.

"That would be nice. What time?" She looked at him under her lashes.

"How about seven? Then we could go stargazing."

"Alone?" She arched her brow.

"No. We'll take Titan. I'm sure he'll love to be your chaperone."

"I'd like that."

CHAPTER 27

"We'll go to Bettie's. It's the best boutique we have in Harland Creek. Be sure to park in the handicap spot. That way I don't have to walk so far." Elizabeth pointed to the store in the square.

"I don't know. Isn't that illegal? I don't have a handicap sticker on my car." She gave Elizabeth a look.

"Honey, people know me and they know I've been riding in your car. They won't say a word," Elizabeth assured her.

"I don't feel right about it." Heather stopped at the parking space and waited.

"Well, how would you feel about me walking two blocks instead of ten feet?" Elizabeth countered.

"Fine. But if we get a ticket, you're paying for it." Heather pulled into the handicap parking spot.

Elizabeth smiled and unbuckled her seat belt. "See. How hard was that?"

"Pretty hard. I'm not used to breaking the law." Heather frowned.

Elizabeth snorted and opened her door.

Heather grabbed her backpack and walked around and helped Elizabeth step onto the curb.

The bell above Bettie's Boutique rang as two women walked out. Heather held the door open for Elizabeth.

"Hello, Miss Elizabeth. Is this your granddaughter with you?" A middle-aged woman stepped out from behind the counter.

"No, Stacey. This is Heather Smith. She's a friend. And we are here to get her a dress. She has a date on Friday night," Elizabeth gushed. "Heather, this is Stacey Landers. She owns the boutique."

Heather forced a smile. She didn't want the whole town knowing her business. "Nice to meet you."

"Nice to meet you. We have some new items that I think you'll love." Stacey smiled brightly.

"Stacey, I need a different size," a customer called out from the back.

"I'll be right there." She turned back to them. "I'll let you both look around, and if you have questions, let me know." She hurried over to a rack and picked off the same dress in a couple of sizes.

"What about this?" Elizabeth held up an animal print dress.

"I don't think so. I don't think it's my style."

"Here's a pretty dress." Elizabeth held up a purple dress with puff sleeves.

"That may be too fancy." Heather bit her lip.

The bell rang as Heather was going through a rack of sale items.

"Look, Heather, this is a nice dress." Elizabeth held up a black dress with long sleeves.

"It's a dinner date. Not a funeral." Heather cocked her head.

"A dinner date? Let me guess with who." Gabriela strolled

over, looking like she'd just stepped off a magazine cover. She wore slim white jeans and a yellow shirt which showed off her body. "Grayson." She smirked and tucked her sunglasses on the top of her head.

"Shush." Heather looked around the boutique. "I don't want the whole town to know."

"It's not like they're not going to know once you guys go to the restaurant." Gabriela shrugged. "Wait, is he taking you to Loftin's?"

"Yes."

A slow smile tugged at her lips. "Then everyone will know by Sunday morning."

"Ugh. Can a girl not have any secrets?" Heather buried her face in the rack of clothes.

"Not here." Gabriela shrugged. She smiled at Elizabeth. "Hello, Ms. Elizabeth. How are you?"

"I'm getting around better. But we are having a hard time figuring out something for Heather to wear. I don't suppose you could help out, since you're the expert?"

"Sure. I'd be happy to." Gabriela quickly went through the clothes and pulled out a black crop top and a short off-white shirt. "This would look great on you."

"That's too short." Elizabeth narrowed her eyes.

Gabriela grinned. "I guess it is." She put the clothes back and went to another rack. "You could wear something like this gray dress. Pair it with some black high heels." She held out a formfitting dress.

"I don't know. That looks pretty tight." Heather cringed.

"You should have come over and looked through my clothes." Gabriela raised her eyebrow.

"I know. I've just been so busy, and well, I feel weird about not paying you."

Gabriela nodded. "Give me a minute." She went through

two racks and finally pulled an outfit together. "How about this?"

She held out a flowy peach-colored skirt and a pretty white blouse. "I would do some simple jewelry like maybe this necklace." She pulled a gold necklace off a mannequin and found some matching earrings on display on the counter. "All you need is some heels. Do you have some nude or maybe black heels?"

"I don't own any heels," Heather admitted.

"Well, don't buy them here. Stacey overprices her shoes." She stared at the owner as she came out of the dressing room.

Heather didn't miss the way Stacey shot daggers at Gabriela.

"I have a pair of nude heels in your size in my car. I was going to donate them. You can have them." Gabriela shrugged. "So what do you think of the outfit?"

Heather smiled. "It's perfect." She looked at Elizabeth. The old woman smiled and nodded.

"Well, go try them on." Elizabeth nudged her.

She stepped into the dressing room and quickly changed into the new clothes. She ran her hand over the soft material. She'd never had new clothes in her life.

"Come on out and let's see how you look," Elizabeth called out.

She opened the dressing room door and stepped out.

"Oh, Heather. You look lovely." Elizabeth's eyes sparkled with emotion. "Do you like the outfit?"

"I do. But it's a lot of money."

"Don't worry about that. It's my treat." Elizabeth nodded.

"Oh no, I can't let you do that." She shook her head.

"Oh yes, you can. Besides, I need people who work for me to look their best when they are on a fancy date." Elizabeth pulled out her wallet.

"Thank you. I appreciate it." Heather blinked back the tears.

"You're welcome."

"Where's Gabriela?" She looked around.

Elizabeth stepped closer. "She and Stacey had words. Gabriela left."

Heather lowered her voice. "Was it over the shoe comment?"

"I couldn't tell. They were too far away. But Gabriela didn't look too pleased. She did say she was putting those shoes in your car."

"I'll have to thank her for that."

"She certainly knows her fashion. That's for sure." Elizabeth patted her hand. "Now go change so we can get these clothes rung up."

Heather went back into the dressing room and quickly changed.

She carefully hung up each item.

New clothes for a new life.

CHAPTER 28

"I can't believe this is happening. Just my luck." Heather turned the key once again. And once again, the engine did nothing.

"Could it be your battery?"

"I don't think so. It was fine yesterday." She turned the key again. Nothing happened.

"I'll run inside and call Gus. He's a mechanic." Elizabeth opened the door.

"Hang on and let me help you." She hurried around the car and assisted Elizabeth inside Bettie's.

Within minutes of making the call to Gus, he was there. For a small town, people moved pretty quickly.

Gus pulled his head out from under the hood. "Sounds like the alternator. Can't really make an official diagnosis until I tow it back to my shop."

"How much is it going to cost to fix it?" Heather groaned.

He grinned. "Well, I won't know until I get her back to my shop and poke around. Could be an easy fix or it could be more expensive."

"Perfect." Heather sighed. "How am I going to get to town without a car?"

"Use my truck. In fact, if I were you, I'd sell it and just drive my truck. That way you can save up and buy some-thing newer. A car is not useful on a farm."

"What would I get?"

"One of those small trucks. A Toyota maybe." Elizabeth shrugged.

Gus scratched his chin. "I might have a buyer for your car. That is, if you want to sell it."

"Really? Who?"

"Well, my grandson. His vehicle was an old beater, and it finally gave up the ghost. He's looking for a car since he's headed to college in the fall."

"Wait, is your grandson Justin?"

"He is. Do you know him?"

"I know he works for Grayson." She nodded.

"Grayson's a good man. He hired my grandson when no one else was hiring." Gus lifted his chin.

"Yes, well, she has a date with Grayson Friday night. That's why we are here shopping." Elizabeth beamed.

"Elizabeth!" Heather glared at her.

"Oh, sorry. I wasn't supposed to tell anyone."

"I tell you what, let me know what's wrong with the car and if your grandson is still interested, tell him to make me an offer."

"I'll do that." Gus grinned from ear to ear.

"Gus, is there any way you can drive us back to the farm?"

"Yes, ma'am. We'll tow the car to the shop, and I'll take you both home in my truck. This is Wednesday so I'll have an idea of what's wrong with it by Friday."

It was after lunch when they arrived back home.

"I'm about worn out. Not sure if it was from all the shopping or the excitement from riding in a tow truck." Elizabeth settled into her chair in the living room.

"Or maybe it was how Gus was flirting with you," Heather teased.

"He was not." Elizabeth scowled. "He's just friendly. That's all."

Heather laughed. "I'll make us a quick lunch. How does chicken salad sandwiches sound?"

"I see you've been practicing expanding your cooking skills." Elizabeth arched her brow.

"I've been watching some cooking shows." She shrugged.

"Good. That's good. Every farmer's wife needs to know how to cook." Elizabeth smirked.

"Whatever." She ignored the comment and took her clothes upstairs to hang them up.

She came back down and made a quick lunch for them. Elizabeth complimented her on the sandwiches, saying they were some of the best ones she'd ever had.

Heather had beamed at the compliment.

She loved cooking. Lately she'd started experimenting with different ingredients.

"I'll do the dishes." Elizabeth stood.

"Are you sure?"

"Yes. Besides, my physical therapist says it's okay." She walked to the sink. "While I'm doing this, go in my room and look at the new quilt pattern I've been working on."

Heather stepped into Elizabeth's bedroom and stopped. She had spread out five blocks of a quilt on her bed. The colors were vibrant against a black background. The pattern was of a star and with the blocks lined up against each other, they looked like stars found in the night sky.

She walked into the kitchen. "They are beautiful. Reminds me of a starry night."

Elizabeth stopped and turned. "The pattern is called

Hunter's Star. I guess it does look like a night sky. You have a good eye."

"Maybe but I definitely can't quilt."

Elizabeth laughed. "Maybe you'll pick it up later in life. You're young. You have your whole life ahead of you."

That night as Heather fell asleep she stared out her window into the night sky, marveling at how much her life had changed in such a short time.

CHAPTER 29

"*D*o you do this for everyone?" Heather tried not to squirm as Gabriela applied the makeup.

"No. But when Ms. Elizabeth called, I couldn't refuse. Plus, I love a good makeover." Gabriela's voice held a tint of excitement.

"Thanks for the shoes. I wanted to tell you the other day, but you had left before I came out of the dressing room."

"Yeah, well, that old bat Stacey didn't appreciate me helping pick out an outfit for you."

"Why? You did a wonderful job. I mean, she should hire you. She'd probably get a ton more customers if she did."

Gabriela stopped. "No, Heather. She wouldn't. No one in Harland Creek will hire me."

Heather wanted to press her for more information, but she could tell by the firm expression Gabriela was done with this conversation.

"Gus called and told me I would need a new alternator. I'm really considering selling the car and saving up for something else. A truck maybe. What do you think?"

"I think if you're staying here a truck would be more

practical. You can't be driving in a pasture in a car. Do you have anyone interested in it?"

"Actually, I do. Gus' grandson. He's looking for a car for college. I told him to make me an offer and get back to me. He's going to run some comps and see what a fair price would be."

"Sounds like you have a plan. And guess what? I'm almost done." Gabriela swiped the lipstick across Heather's lips and took a step back.

"You look beautiful." She nodded.

"I do?" Heather had never heard those words before.

"Yes. And if Grayson McCade is too stupid to tell you that, then I would drop him like a hot potato."

"I don't think Grayson is stupid." Heather defended him.

A slow smile crept across her mouth. "Neither do I. Now turn and look in the mirror."

She stood from the chair and turned around to look in the mirror above the dresser.

She gasped.

"I'm guessing that's a good gasp and not a horrified gasp." Gabriela cocked her head.

"I look beautiful." Her makeup had been tastefully applied. The bronze pallet of eyeshadow accentuated her blue eyes and the blush highlighted her cheekbones. Even her light-pink lipstick made her lips look perfect. Gabriela had used a curler and given her beach waves which fell across her shoulders. She never imagined she could look like this.

"You've always been beautiful. I just shone a spotlight." Gabriela shrugged and began gathering up her supplies. "I need to get going. Agnes has it in her head for me to help her with those dang beehives."

Heather turned and gave Gabriela a quick hug. "Thank you."

145

Gabriela gave her an uneasy look and ducked her head. "No problem. I just want all the juicy details after the date."

Heather snorted. "There won't be any juicy details. It will probably bore you."

"I like boring." Gabriela grabbed her bag and stopped. "Oh, one more thing. Don't take that ugly backpack."

"What's wrong with my backpack?" Heather scowled.

"First of all, you're not fourteen anymore, nor are you in school. You need a proper purse. I brought you one. It's not new but it will do until you can get one you really like." She pulled out a small black purse.

"Where am I going to put all my stuff?" She frowned.

"You don't need to be carrying your stuff around on your back like a turtle. All you need is the basics. Your driver's license, money and credit card, and your keys. Well, since your car's not running, you don't even need that. Oh, and you'll need your lipstick." She slung her bag on her arm. "Now go have fun."

Gabriela disappeared out the door.

Heather took another look at herself. She still had to get dressed. She glanced at the clock on the bedside table, noting the time. Grayson would be here any minute.

She quickly began to get dressed for her very first date.

CHAPTER 30

"That was the best meal I've ever eaten." She sighed and sat back in her chair.

"Loftin's is the only place to get a good steak in Harland Creek." He took a sip of his iced tea. "Do you feel like desert?"

"I couldn't eat another thing." She shook her head.

"You look beautiful." Grayson couldn't keep his eyes off Heather.

She ducked her head. "You told me that already."

"I'm telling you again."

She looked up at him. "You know I don't normally look like this. And I'm probably not going to start wearing makeup to work on the flower farm."

He laughed. "You could wear a gunny sack and still look beautiful."

She frowned. "What's a gunny sack?"

He laughed again. "I have one hanging up in my barn. I'll show you before we go stargazing."

Her eyes widened. "Stargazing. I completely forgot. I should have brought a change of clothes."

"Don't worry about it. We can stop by your house and you can change. You didn't think I was going to be dressed like this all night, did you?"

She laughed and relaxed.

"That looks good on you."

"Gabriela picked out the outfit." She glanced down.

"I wasn't talking about the outfit. I was talking about the smile."

"I guess I have a lot to smile about. A new home and a job I like. I never thought I would find those things."

He took her hand in his. "Heather, I…"

"Grayson, I'm sorry to interrupt your date." Sloan stopped at the table and looked down at him.

She pulled her hand away and took a sip of water.

"Sloan, you remember Heather from church."

"Hello again, Heather." Sloan didn't smile but had kept his demeanor professional.

"Is everything okay?" Grayson frowned. Unease snaked in his belly. "It's not Olivia, is it?"

"No, no. As far as I know she's fine. Actually, I'm not here to see you. I'm here to see Heather." He kept his gaze on her.

"Me?" She frowned, looking confused.

"Yes. It's about the car that was towed to Gus' shop. Apparently, when he ran the VIN number to get some comps to determine the value of the car for resell, the car came back flagged."

"What does that mean?"

"It means that the car was reported stolen in Georgia. I'm going to need you to come with me to the station to answer some questions."

"Stolen! I didn't steal that car. There must be some mistake." Her eyes widened. She looked very much like a cornered animal.

"I've got Elizabeth in the car with me. I went to the farm

to speak to you, and she insisted on coming with me to find you."

"I see." Her face turned pale and she gripped the corner of the table as she stood.

"I'm going too." Grayson stood and waved the waitress over. He handed her some money for the meal. "I'll drive her to the station."

"I'm afraid you can't do that." Sloan gave him a tense look.

"What are you saying? You just going to throw her in the back of the car like a common criminal?"

When Sloan didn't answer, Grayson realized that's exactly what he was going to do.

"Sloan..."

Heather pressed her trembling hand to his chest. "Grayson, it's okay. I'll go. I don't want to make a bigger deal out of this than it already is. People are starting to look."

He glanced at the restaurant where patrons had gathered at the window to peer out.

She was already getting into the back seat of Sloan's patrol car.

His stomach clenched. Something about all this wasn't right.

He jumped in his truck and sped over to the police station. By the time he got there, Sloan was escorting Heather and Elizabeth into a small room.

Sloan put his hand on his chest when he tried to enter. "I'm sorry, Grayson, but I have to follow procedure."

"Sloan, forget your procedure."

Sloan glared and let him enter.

Heather was sitting in the only chair across the table from Sloan. Elizabeth and Grayson stood behind her.

"Is your name Heather Smith? From Atlanta, Georgia?"

"Yes." Her voice was small in the room.

"Heather, can you tell me how you came to be in possession of the car?" Sloan cocked his head.

"Mrs. Ruth Galloway gave me the car."

"And is she a relative?"

"No." She shook her head.

"Is she someone you worked for?"

"Kind of." She clasped her hands in her lap.

Sloan sighed. "So you're saying a Mrs. Galloway gave you her car without any money changing hands? And you barely knew her and you were not related?"

"Well, yes."

"Heather if you were in my shoes, wouldn't you find that hard to believe?"

"But she did give it to me. I have proof."

"Do you have a title to the car?"

"I have the paperwork in my backpack. It's back at the farm." She glanced back at Elizabeth.

"I'll run and fetch it." Elizabeth nodded.

Grayson shook his head. "I'll go. You still can't climb the stairs, remember?"

"Fine. But I'm going too." She clasped Heather on the shoulder. "We'll hurry back and get this all cleared up."

"We'll hurry. Okay?" He looked into Heather's scared eyes.

She said nothing but nodded.

He could tell her faith in the situation was quickly waning.

CHAPTER 31

*G*rayson took the stairs two at a time. He turned and opened the door to Heather's room.

Her backpack was nowhere to be seen. He went to the closet and opened it up. The few clothes she had were hung neatly on hangers. Her sneakers were the only item on the top shelf. He knelt and spotted her black backpack on the floor. He picked it up and found a stash of nonperishable food behind it.

Why would she be storing food?

Unease snaked up his spine. He grabbed the backpack and dumped the contents out on the bed.

Toothbrush, toothpaste, a lollipop, phone charger, a change of clothes, a recipe book, a map with small towns circled, an envelope, and a roll of money poured onto the bed.

Why would she be hiding money in her backpack instead of putting it in the bank?

His heart beat a little bit faster as he opened the envelope.

He pulled out the official title to the car.

His stomach hit the floor.

Ruth Galloway still owned the car. She never signed the car over to Heather.

The food, the money, the title.

It all made sense now.

He forked his fingers through his hair and hurried down the stairs with the title in his hand.

"Grayson, did you find it?" Elizabeth called from the kitchen.

"Yes. I'm headed back to the station."

"Wait and I'll go with you."

"No. You stay here."

"But, Grayson, Heather needs me there."

He stopped, his hand on the doorknob. "Ms. Elizabeth, I'm afraid to tell you. But Heather is not who she says she is."

"How can you say that?" Elizabeth berated.

He spun around and faced the old woman. "Because she has a stash of food, a roll of cash, and the title of the car isn't in her name. I'm sorry to say she's been lying to all of us."

He hurried out of the house and down the steps before she could defend her.

He white-knuckled the steering wheel as he drove back into town.

CHAPTER 32

"*I* brought you some coffee. Sorry, we're out of creamer." Sloan set the Styrofoam cup in front of her.

"Thanks," she said softly. She lifted the hot coffee to her lips and sipped. She grimaced at the strong taste.

"Sorry. Should have warned you about that. Cooper makes the coffee strong."

She nodded. Just when she thought everything was going great, this happens.

She should have known not to get her hopes up.

She should have known not to let her guard down.

She should have known she'd never have a home here.

There was a knock on the window. She jerked her head in that direction and saw Grayson standing there. He didn't look at her but motioned for Sloan.

"I'll be right back. Hopefully we can get this cleared up."

The door slammed behind him and she jumped.

She didn't like it here. It was too cramped and dark.

A few minutes later Sloan reappeared with an envelope in his hand.

"Where's Grayson?"

"He had to leave. Technically, he can't be here."

Her stomach dropped. "You're being too nice, Sloan. He left because he doesn't believe me."

He pressed his lips into a thin line. "You know it's better for everyone if you just be honest."

"You don't believe me." She pushed the coffee away and clasped her hands in her lap.

"Not when I have evidence like this."

"Like what?" She frowned.

"Grayson found the title to the car in your backpack. The title still has Ruth Galloway as the owner of the car. If she had given it to you, then she would have signed it over to you." He sat down on the other side of the table.

"I didn't know that. I have never had a car before."

"And there's more."

"What are you talking about?"

"Grayson found your backpack in your closet with a wad of money, along with items that look like you were ready to leave at a moment's notice."

"I've always had a backpack. I've moved around so much I never really had a place long enough to call home. I guess it's just habit. It doesn't mean I was getting ready to run off."

"And the money?" He cocked his eyes.

"I cashed my checks from Elizabeth. I don't have a bank account yet."

He sighed heavily. "And the food. He said he found food stashed in your closet."

She felt like she was sitting here naked in front of the police officer. Vulnerable and exposed.

She crossed her arms and gritted her teeth.

Old familiar walls rose up around her and she refused to talk.

"Okay, I'm going to need you to stay here until I talk to

the authorities in Georgia and see what the family wants to do. Right now, the family is getting ready to auction off her home and belongings and won't be available until tomorrow morning."

"I'm spending the night in jail?" Fear thudded in her chest.

"Yes." Sloan stood and opened the door.

Her legs felt like lead as she stood and walked into the hallway.

He led her to one of three jail cells in the building. He opened the door of the empty cell.

"If she goes in, then I am too." Olivia appeared in the hallway.

"Olivia, you need to go home." Sloan sighed. "Grayson's already been here."

"He left?" She glared. "Wait until I talk to my brother."

"Olivia, you can't be back here."

"Well, I'm not going anywhere. If she's getting locked up, then lock me up too."

"Aren't you afraid I'm a hardened criminal?" Heather narrowed her eyes.

"No. And I know people. I'm not wrong about people." She pursed her lips. "Most of the time."

"Olivia…"

"I think there's some kind of rule around about having a female chaperone for a female prisoner. I mean, you don't want a lawsuit on your hands if she sues you for sexual harassment, or…"

"Fine!" Sloan glared. "You can stay. But you have to leave any personal items with me."

"You can keep my purse but you're not keeping my cookies from the bakery." She held up the bag. "Women need chocolate in times of stress. And during menstruation."

Sloan paled and quickly ushered the women in the cell and locked it behind them.

When they could no longer hear his footsteps, Olivia sat down on the bottom bunk. "Sit."

Heather felt the sting of tears behind her eyes and tried to blink them away. When she sat down, she felt Olivia's arms pull her into a hug. She lost all control, letting the tears stain her face.

CHAPTER 33

"*I*'m sorry. I didn't mean to fall apart like that." Heather swiped at the tears on her cheeks.

"Here. Sloan was so upset that I said menstruation that he forgot to get my purse." She pulled out a Kleenex and handed it to her.

"Thanks." She smiled a little. "Smart thinking about that."

"Yes. Men are so easily distracted." Olivia brightened.

"You shouldn't be here, Olivia. Grayson is going to think I'm trying to turn you against him."

She narrowed her eyes. "Grayson has a lot of explaining to do. He should have stayed here and supported you. Instead of running when he got scared."

"That's not exactly what happened." Heather sighed. "How did you know I was here? Does the whole town know already?" She buried her face in her hands.

"Relax. Have a cookie and tell me what's really going on. Elizabeth was the one who called and told me what you are being accused of. She asked if I could come and see if you need anything."

"She did?" Heather's eyes burned with fresh tears.

"Yes. Now don't start crying again. A cookie will help that." She pulled one of out the bakery bag and handed it to her.

"Thanks." She took a bite. "These are good."

"They are the best in town. Now tell me what's going on."

Heather swallowed and took a deep breath. "They think I stole a car..."

Olivia shook her head. "I know that. I want to know your side of the story. How did you get the car? Start from there."

She nodded. "Okay. I don't know if Grayson told you, but I grew up in foster care. So I don't have any family."

"I didn't know. Grayson didn't say anything to me." Olivia squeezed her arm.

"I was working at a dry cleaner in Atlanta. Because I worked extra hours, my boss put a cot in the back room for me to spend the night when I worked late. The thing was, I worked late all the time. So I basically lived there. He never said anything, but I think he knew. He put a small refrigerator and coffee pot in the room. Anyway, we had this customer, Mrs. Ruth Galloway who would come in every week. I got to know her and we would chat. Sometimes she would bring me goodies like cookies or muffins. She was always telling me I was too thin." She smiled as she recalled her old friend. "One week she didn't come in. She called the owner and asked if her cleaning could be delivered. She had a weak spell and had fallen. She was scared to drive. Her children didn't live near and she really didn't have anyone to help her. She was friends with the owner, and he allowed me to drive the company car to take her stuff to her every week. We would have tea and cookies and talk for fifteen minutes before I would have to go back to work. One day she asked me if I ever considered becoming a caregiver. I hadn't. She offered me a job to come live with her and take care of her. She said she knew I was living at the dry cleaner. She said this would be a good thing for both of us. She would have a caretaker and I would have a home."

"She sounds like a lovely woman." Olivia smiled and took a cookie.

"She was." Heather cleared her throat. "She gave me the keys to her car. She said I would need to have transportation to drive her around. She said she would put it in her will that I was to get the car when she passed. She said all the insurance paperwork and title were in the glove compartment of her car. Anyway, I gave my two weeks' notice and started driving the car whenever I dropped her clothes off. While I was there, I would do laundry, clean her house, and help her write some letters to her relatives. She would always tell me to have dreams and goals. She would make me promise her that I would find out what I wanted in life and go for it. I told her I would. Someone had taken my position at the dry cleaner and I was just showing them the ropes until I left so I was working part-time there. I had also started living with her. It was nice to have a home and my own bedroom."

"I'm sure it was. Every girl needs their own space," Olivia agreed.

"One day, I went to wake her. And she had died in her sleep." Heather swallowed hard at the memory of her friend.

"I called the ambulance and the police showed up. They all agreed she'd probably had a stroke. She died peacefully and without pain."

Heather shook her head. "I was so upset. The family wanted me out of the house immediately. Honestly, I didn't want to be there myself. Anyway, I packed my meager belongings in the car and drove around for a while. I ended up sleeping in my car a few nights. She had died before paying me, so all I had was the money left over from working at the dry cleaner. One night I slept in the parking lot of the library. When a cop banged on my window at six in the morning asking what I was doing, I lied and said I was waiting for the library to open. He hung around. So when the library opened, I went in. I ended up at the computer section and researched the best places to live. I wanted small town, family friendly, and low cost of living. I ended up coming across Harland Creek, Mississippi. And that's when I searched the want ads. I found Elizabeth's job posting for a caretaker. So I applied and got an interview." Heather shook her head. "I didn't steal the car."

"I know you didn't. Ruth probably just forgot to sign it over to you before she died," Olivia said softly.

"And now Grayson thinks I'm a liar."

"Grayson can be an idiot sometimes." Olivia shook her head.

"You don't understand. He found my backpack with money in it. And my stash of food."

"Stash of food?" Olivia frowned.

"It's embarrassing."

"I'm not judging," Olivia assured her.

"I keep a stash of food, usually nonperishables, in my bedroom. It became a habit. When you are in foster care, not all the homes are good ones. Sometimes you don't know when you will get your next meal. So I keep things like peanut butter and granola bars, things that have a long shelf life in my room. Just in case." She shrugged.

"Heather, I'm so sorry. I can't imagine growing up like that." Olivia shoved the whole bag of cookies at her. "Here. Take all of them."

Heather laughed and shook her head. "It's okay. I know I'm not going to starve."

"Is there anything else, anywhere that Ruth would have written a new will or her intentions down?" Olivia pressed.

"Not that I know of. The only time I saw her writing was

when she was writing to her distant relatives and taking notes when she'd watch a preacher on TV."

"Don't give up. I believe you." Olivia smiled.

"Thank you. You're the only one that does." Heather felt the weight of the world.

"Well, might as well make these bunks up so we can get some sleep."

"You can't stay here, Olivia." Heather shook her head.

"I'm not going anywhere. We'll figure this all out in the morning." She nodded. "Oh, I almost forgot." She opened her purse and pulled out something wrapped in a paper towel.

"It's not a bouquet, but I picked it in my yard before I came over." She held out the single daisy to her.

"Thank you." Heather took it.

"We all need some beauty in our lives, especially when times look the darkest."

That night as Heather tried to sleep, she stared at the daisy lying beside her on the pillow.

Hopefully dawn would look a lot different than the bleak night.

CHAPTER 34

*G*rayson didn't sleep that night. He stayed on the computer and looked up anything he could regarding Ruth Galloway. He came across Ruth's obituary and tried to track down her family. Most lived outside the state of Georgia. But after all night, he did track down the son who gave him an earful at six in the morning for calling so early.

"Again, I'm sorry for calling so early, but it's important. I'm in Harland Creek, Mississippi, and I need some information on someone your mother knew."

"Well, I'm trying to get my mother's estate sale ready for today. I don't know who you are but you have awful timing," Richard Galloway barked into the phone.

"Please don't hang up. It's important. It's about Heather Smith."

"Oh. Her. I suppose this is about what we discovered yesterday. My attorney was supposed to be handling those details for me and getting in contact with the local authorities."

"Mr. Galloway, I don't think Heather stole your mother's car…"

"Of course she didn't. We found my mother's updated will in her Bible while we were getting things ready for the sale. My attorney realizes my mother intended to sign over the car to Heather. In the will she states upon her death she gets the car. She stated that Heather took care of her more than her children did. I don't necessarily agree but that's not the point. My attorney said he would handle everything today. I'm sorry for any inconvenience this has caused the girl. Now I really have to go." Richard hung up the phone.

Relief and joy washed over him.

She was innocent.

He jumped in the shower. As he dressed, he hoped that Heather would forgive him for ever doubting her.

He raced to the police station, not caring that he was breaking the speed limit. He needed to get to Heather. He needed to apologize.

He parked in front of the station and ran up the steps.

"Where's Sloan?" he asked the receptionist.

"He's in a meeting." She looked at him over her glasses.

"I need to see him; its important," Grayson demanded.

"It's okay, Shelly." Sloan appeared in the hallway. "If you are looking for Heather, she's gone."

"You mean released," Grayson corrected him. "She was wrongfully accused of something she didn't do. The woman's son…"

"I know. Found the updated will in the Bible. It's all cleared up," Sloan reassured him.

"Did she go back to Elizabeth's?"

"I don't know. She and Olivia left at the same time."

"Olivia?"

"Yes. She insisted on spending the night in the slammer

with Heather." Sloan narrowed his eyes. "She can be quite convincing when she wants to be." He turned and headed back to his office.

CHAPTER 35

*H*eather waved to Olivia as she drove away from Elizabeth's house. She glanced down at her wrinkled skirt and shirt and sighed. With her heels in her hand, she walked up the steps to the front door.

"Heather, I was so worried about you." Elizabeth was there, wearing a bright-yellow muumuu, her hair going every which way.

"I'm okay. The police cleared everything up."

"Good. Now come in the kitchen and let's talk."

Her stomach dropped. Elizabeth was going to give her the talk about how this isn't working out and how she couldn't possibly stay there anymore.

She didn't have it in her to argue. Defeated, she followed Elizabeth into the kitchen where the smell of coffee hung in the air.

"I just made a fresh pot. Been up all night. I heard Olivia spent the night with you. She's a good girl, that Olivia."

"Who told you that?" She frowned.

"Sloan did. He called and asked me if I could talk her out of it." She snorted. "I told him no. And he was no longer going to get any more apple pies from me on the Fourth of July."

"Elizabeth, he apologized. He said it was a mix-up…"

"I know, I know. That's not what I want to talk about." She set a cup of coffee and cream and sugar in front of her. She poured herself a cup and sat across from her.

"You didn't tell me you came out of the foster system."

"I was afraid you wouldn't hire me if you knew."

"That's the dumbest thing I've ever heard. I just want you to be honest with me."

"Okay. I came out of the foster system. I don't have a bank account so I cash my checks and keep a wad of cash in my backpack. I have always had a backpack since I was eight. Before then I carried my clothes from house to house in a garbage bag until someone donated one to me. In a way, I live out of it. I always have. I also keep food in my room out of habit."

"Food insecure." She nodded and sipped her coffee. "I get it."

"Really?"

"Yes. Donna's daughter adopted a son who came out of the foster care system. She would find boxes of crackers and cereal hidden under his bed."

"It makes me feel secure in a way." She shrugged and sipped her coffee. "This is way better than jail coffee." She put her coffee mug down. "Look, I appreciate everything you've done for me. If you'll just let me shower, I can pack my stuff and get out of your way."

Elizabeth gave her a shocked look. "Leave? Why would you leave?"

"I lied about who I was."

"Heather, you are human. The Bible says we are to forgive. What kind of Christian would I be if I didn't forgive?"

Heather sat there looking at her, too stunned to speak.

"Now, you finish that coffee. I'm making eggs and bacon and grits…"

"Wait. I don't understand. Are you asking me to stay? What if your children don't want me here? What if something happens…"

"What if something happens to me? I've already handled all that. I talked to all my children last night. None of them want the responsibility of the flower farm. They all agreed to let you stay on and live here to help me with it. If something does happen to me, which it won't because I feel as fit as a bull, then you will be allowed to stay in the house and farm the land for as long as you want. The children will still inherit the land and if they want to sell it, they have to give you the first right of refusal. But they can't sell it until ten years after I'm dead. That will give you enough time to come up with money to buy it if you want. Or maybe you'll be living on the farm next door as the farmer's wife." She waggled her eyebrows.

"I doubt that. Grayson never wants to see me again."

"Oh, I wouldn't be so sure. I talked to him this morning. He was up all night, calling every Galloway in the directory. He talked to the son and found out everything this morning. He called from the jail when he realized you were not there."

"Really? I'm not sure how I feel about that."

"You feel how you want to feel. Hurt, angry, unsure. You got plenty of time to figure it out. Now go upstairs and get cleaned up, and then we'll eat."

CHAPTER 36

Grayson hurried up the front steps of Elizabeth's house. The scent of bacon reminded him he hadn't eaten breakfast.

He rapped on the screen door.

"You stay put. I'll answer it," Elizabeth insisted.

He wanted to barge in, but he knew neither Elizabeth nor Heather would appreciate that. Not after how he had treated her last night.

"Grayson. I should say I'm surprised to see you, but I'd be lying." Elizabeth held the door open for him. "She's in the kitchen."

He stopped in his tracks. "What if she doesn't want to see me?"

"She probably doesn't."

He hesitated. "But I want to see her. I need to apologize."

Elizabeth nodded.

"She probably never wants to see me again."

"You should ask yourself two questions, Grayson. What do you want? And are you willing to fight for it?"

She was right. Elizabeth usually was. He nodded and made his way to the kitchen.

Heather was sitting there dressed in her usual yellow T-shirt and jeans. Her hair hung in wet tendrils around her face. She stared into her cup of coffee as he sat at the table.

"Heather, I need to apologize. I'm sorry for not believing you. I should have had more faith in you. And for that I'm so sorry. When I got home, I realized what a mistake I had made. I was willing to let go of someone I care about because I was afraid of being hurt again. Of being deceived. It made me realize you are not Sarah. And it made me realize I don't deserve you."

She set her cup down. "Grayson, I had a lot of time to think last night. And I realized that I do deserve better in life. I want someone who will fight for me and trust me and never let me down. At the same time, I think you have kept your walls up and not been vulnerable. I know it's scary to let someone in, but the other option is being alone forever."

He cleared his throat. "You are probably right. You've been right about a lot of things. I may be older, but you are wiser than me."

"I agree with that." She took a sip of her coffee. "I do forgive you, Grayson, but right now, I need to be by myself, to figure things out."

"You're not leaving, are you?" His heart dropped.

"Leaving? Are you crazy?" Elizabeth walked into the kitchen. "She's going to officially be caretaker of the farm. I'm talking to my attorney about putting it in writing. This week, in fact."

"That's great." He felt like he could breathe again.

"Sounds like you've got some making up to do," Elizabeth muttered.

"So there's hope?" he asked.

"There's always hope." She lifted her eyes to him.

It cut him to the core to see how red her eyes had been from crying.

"I'll do whatever it takes to prove how much you mean to me, Heather." He stood and headed out the front door.

Elizabeth grinned.

"Why are you smiling?"

"I've never seen him like that. I'm curious to see how he's going to make it up to you. I bet he'll bring you a bouquet and candy."

Heather laughed. "Maybe. But I still need time too. I meant it when I said I needed time."

"Right." Elizabeth snorted. "We'll see how much time you need."

CHAPTER 37

*T*hat afternoon, a large bouquet of red roses was delivered to Heather at the farm. Elizabeth crowed over her astute guess.

Heather glanced at the gifts and headed out to check on the flowers. She liked that the chores of the farm took her mind off Grayson.

The next day a large box was delivered by Gabriela. "This is from Grayson. I picked them out and he paid for them." She leaned closer. "Don't worry. I made him buy the most expensive chocolates they had."

"I can't keep these." Heather shook her head.

"Oh yes, you can. I'll call Agnes over, and we'll all eat them together," Elizabeth said.

On the third day, Grayson changed his course. Instead of chocolates and roses, he sent her a dozen potted herbs.

"What an odd gift." Elizabeth frowned.

"No, not at all. He knows I'm learning to cook. These will come in handy. This is something I will definitely enjoy." She turned to Elizabeth. "How do you feel about cilantro?"

"I'm not a fan." Elizabeth scowled.

"You will be when I use it in a soup." Heather gathered her herbs and carefully placed them on the windowsills in the kitchen.

On day four, Grayson left a package on the front porch. When Heather opened the screen door to step out, she almost tripped over it. The note, like the other gifts before, simply said, Forgive me.

She carefully untied the box and lifted the lid. Sitting inside was a very sleepy baby goat.

"Elizabeth! Look!" She burst into the kitchen holding the baby.

"What in the world? It's a goat?" Elizabeth blinked over her coffee. "What is Grayson McCade thinking?"

"I love it." She nuzzled the kid under her chin.

"Heather, where are we going to keep that thing?" Elizabeth scowled.

"I don't know. Can't I keep it in my room?"

Elizabeth shook her head.

On the fifth day, Grayson showed up around five that afternoon. Heather had just come in from watering the flowers. Her boots were muddy; her hair was sweaty, and she was carrying her baby goat in her arms.

"That goat isn't going to learn how to walk if you keep carrying him like that."

She stopped in her tracks. "I can't let him down when I go water the flowers. He tries to eat them."

"Goats do that." Grayson grinned.

"I got the other gifts as well. I'm sorry I haven't thanked you for them. Agnes and Elizabeth ate most of the chocolates though. But the herbs I'm using every night when I cook dinner."

"I thought you'd like them." He nodded. "I just want you to know I think about you all the time. And when I sleep, I think about you too."

She swallowed.

"Well, I just thought you should know." He raked his hand through his hair and turned.

"Grayson, wait."

He turned slowly. "Yes."

"I do forgive you." The words tumbled out of her mouth.

"You do?" His eyes shone with hope.

"Yes. But you need to know that I want to take things slowly."

"Of course. I can do that." He stepped close. The baby goat bleated and gnawed on his shirt.

"Are you sure? I think we need to have a conversation about what we want as far as long-term goals." Heather looked up at him.

"I already know what I want. I want you and no one else. If I have to wait twenty years until you're ready to commit to me, then I'll wait. You know, in one of my dreams I saw you on my front porch waving me in for dinner. That's what I want. I want to make a home with you. And we will take as much time as you need."

Her heart swelled and burst with joy. "Are you sure about that?"

"I'm positive. I would like to ask you on another date. Since this is Saturday, I would love to sit next to you at church tomorrow."

She grinned and touched his cheek. "Okay, but you have to run it by Elizabeth first. She's very protective of me these days."

"As she should be. As she should."

THE END.

173

ABOUT THE AUTHOR

Jodi Allen Brice has written numerous books under a different pen name. Under Jodi Allen Brice she writes fiction and small town clean and sweet romance.

She transitioned away from paranormal romance in the year 2020 when the virus hit. She said she felt she needed to write a book that would change hearts and minds where Christ is concerned. She is a Christian who loves studying Bible prophesy and spending time with her family in Arkansas. She's is also an avid quilter and camping. Sometimes she does both at the same time!

Her favorite Bible verse is I Corinthians 15:51-52

"In a flash, in the twinkling of an eye, at the last trumpet. For the trumpet will sound, the dead will be raised imperishable, and we will be changed."

John 3:16 "For God so loved the world that he gave his one and only son, so whosoever believes in Him shall not perish but have eternal life."

Check out her website at http://jodiallenbrice.com

f

ALSO BY JODI ALLEN BRICE

Novels

So This Is goodbye

Harland Creek Series
Promise Kept
Promise Made
Promise Forever

Made in the USA
Las Vegas, NV
21 July 2021